Praise for *Sunday You Learn How to Box*

"*Sunday You Learn How to Box* has all the rhythm, drama, and dance of a good fight but in this case the battle matters more because the soul of a boy is at stake. In elegant and agile prose, Wright matches brutality with passion and heartbreak with hope. And a man in purple polyester pants walks off with the prize. This book is a knockout."

—KARIN COOK, author of *What Girls Learn*

"A mother's uphill battle to forge a better life for her family, her young son's struggle to survive in a world where the lines of 'manhood' and 'masculinity' are harshly drawn—Bil Wright's wrenching novel about growing up gay is sometimes crushing, sometimes exhilarating, but always full of grace. In this elegant and honest book, Wright engages difficult themes of love exhausted and renewed, dreams derailed and put back on track again, and the stubborn will to create one's destiny instead of falling prey to it. I was powerfully moved by *Sunday You Learn How to Box*. Its images singe. Its characters gleam."

—GERRY GOMEZ PEARLBERG,
author of *Marianne Fauthfull's Cigarette*
and editor of *Queer Dog: Homo/Pup/Poetry*

"*Sunday You Learn How to Box* is smart and sexy. Bil Wright's gorgeous first novel overflows with wit and lyricism, the wonders of desire, and the brutality of racism. Louis shows us the power of salvation when the savior and saved are one—I couldn't put it down!"

—STEPHANIE GRANT, author of *The Passion of Alice*

SUNDAY YOU LEARN HOW TO BOX

A NOVEL

Bil Wright

SCRIBNER PAPERBACK FICTION
PUBLISHED BY SIMON & SCHUSTER
NEW YORK   LONDON   SYDNEY   SINGAPORE

SCRIBNER PAPERBACK FICTION
Simon & Schuster, Inc.
Rockefeller Center
1230 Avenue of the Americas
New York, NY 10020

This book is a work of fiction. Names, characters, places, and incidents
either are products of the author's imagination or are used fictitiously.
Any resemblance to actual events or locales or persons, living or dead,
is entirely coincidental.

SCRIBNER PAPERBACK FICTION and design are trademarks of Macmillan
Library Reference USA, Inc., used under license by Simon & Schuster,
the publisher of this work.

DESIGNED BY ERICH HOBBING

Manufactured in the United States of America

1   3   5   7   9   10   8   6   4   2

Library of Congress Cataloging-in-Publication Data
Wright, Bil.
Sunday you learn how to box : a novel / Bil Wright.
1. Afro-Americans—Connecticut Fiction. I. Title.
PS3573.R4938S8   2000
813'.54—dc21   99-41479
CIP

ISBN 0-684-85795-2

ACKNOWLEDGMENTS

Thank you God for the journey. Thank you to the following for their encouragement: Becket Logan, Paula West, Traci West, Robynne West, Jerry Watts, Rick Northcutt, Antonio Suarez, Karen Amore, Edna Davis, Kathleen Connolly, John Edward McGrath, Sharon van Ivan, Michael Campbell, Bob Najjar, Linda Herring, Margret McBride, The Millay Colony, the Edward F. Albee Foundation. Thanks to Winifred Golden for her belief from the beginning and to Cherise Grant for being a wise and caring eye.

SUNDAY
YOU LEARN
HOW TO
BOX

1

1968

Mom and I were both sure Ben was dead. If I'm never sure of anything else in my life, I knew the exact moment Ben and I had stopped speaking to each other for good. And I knew Mom could tell he wasn't listening to her anymore, either.

Ben was on the driver's side, Mom was in the middle, next to him. I was squeezed up against the door. There should have been more room, since none of us was what you'd call big. When I was eight and first saw Ben, he looked like a craggy mountain with long arms. He was tall alright, about six three or four maybe, but he had no stomach, no hilly butt like a lot of black men have. By the time he died, he didn't look like a mountain at all. He was more like a high pile of rocks. Mom was short and small like me. But that Sunday, she had on a handmedown fur coat she called "the grizzly" that took up most of the front seat.

When we heard the siren, Mom put her head on Ben's shoulder and her arm around him like you see teenage girls doing with their boyfriends when they cruise past you on the highway. The difference was, Ben was Mom's second husband and I'd never seen her sit next to him that way before, anywhere.

It couldn't have been more than twenty-five degrees outside, but inside Ben's car it felt like there was a bonfire in the backseat. Mom and I were sweating. I'd even seen water running from Ben's mustache along the top of his lip when she was pounding on him. He'd sneered at us like he always did when Mom and I were going crazy, but his forehead was shiny and wet looking, which was different for him. The three of us had been in plenty of fights and Mom and I would be dripping afterwards like we'd been pushed underwater with all our clothes on. But Ben never looked any different at the end than he had at the beginning. The first time I remember seeing him sweat was the Sunday he died.

The cops came screeching into the projects parking lot and blocked Ben's car. One of them ran over, threw open the door on my side and jumped back with his hand on his gun. A freezing wind blew in on all of us. The world was larger, again, than the inside of Ben's Pontiac.

I hadn't even heard the radio. One of us must've kicked or knocked into it accidentally during the fight. Martha and the Vandellas were singing "Jimmy Mack," which meant it was on a station Ben wouldn't have approved of. He didn't usually allow the radio to be played at all, because he said it wore down the battery. When he did turn it on, the only station we could listen to was the one that played music from the thirties and forties. I'd asked Ben once why that was. He'd frowned into the rear-view mirror. "You think I'm going to argue about what to play on the radio in a car I bought with *my* money? When you buy your *own* car, buddy, you can play all the stations at the same time if you want to."

"C'mon now, c'mon!" the cop ordered us with his hand still on his gun. I pushed out staring at the ground, shivering. Mom came behind me, gasping like she was drowning. She opened the grizzly, trying to pull me inside, but I jerked away. No matter how cold I was, I wouldn't let her wrap me up under her coat like some baby faggot kangaroo. If they were going to accuse anybody of killing Ben, I wanted them to think it could've been me as much as her.

By the time the cops got there, just about everybody who lived in the projects was in the parking lot. A lot of them had circled the car and watched us, so there were plenty of witnesses eager to tell what they'd seen. When we'd stopped fighting and Ben was sitting there without the sneer on his face anymore, Isabelle Jackson, the girl from next door, put her nose up against the window and whined to Mom, "Mrs. Ben, you can't get out?" She ran to tell her mother, who called the police to report a man had just murdered his wife in the Stratfield Projects parking lot. Once they got there, the police didn't seem to care that the details they'd been given were wrong.

"Jimmy Mack" was over. The announcer was saying if he got enough calls he'd play "Sittin' on the Dock of the Bay" by Otis Redding. "If you remember one song from this year, I betcha it'll be this one," he said. "Dial my number, kids, and tell me you wanna hear it. Call Uncle Davie and tell him how bad you want ol' Otis to sing that song."

When the ambulance arrived, one of the men examined Ben, listened to Mom's version of what she called an argument and told the police Ben probably had a heart attack. They had trouble pulling him out of the car because he was so long. Every time his head thumped against the steering wheel or the door, Mom winced and whispered, "God. Oh, God." When they got him onto the stretcher, she grabbed for me again, making an appeal to the cops. "We have to go back. My baby girl's alone."

It was true we'd left my sister Lorelle behind, but she

was five years old and no one including Mom ever called her a baby anymore. At first, it looked like they weren't going to let her go. She began to sob. The sobs seemed to be coming from somewhere deep inside the grizzly, getting louder with each breath. People from the projects backed away like they didn't know what Mom would do next, but reasoned it was better to give her some room, just in case.

"Where's your baby, lady?" one of the cops asked her. "I'll go with you."

Mom apologized to me over her shoulder as the two of them started toward the apartment. "I'll be back, Louis. I will." That left me alone with the gun-happy cop, the gawkers from the projects and the ambulance men banging Ben's body around. The Fifth Dimension had just started "Stoned Soul Picnic" when the cop reached in and finally turned the car radio off. Now Ben's battery had been wasted on Martha and the Vandellas, Otis Redding and The Fifth Dimension.

With everybody from the projects staring, waiting to see whether I'd be dragged away in handcuffs, I couldn't tell whether it was the cold or my nerves making me twitch. I focused hard on a broken Coke bottle frozen in the ice, concentrating on the curves in the glass and the part of the letter C that was left, trying to control my shaking.

Somebody called my name. Although it sounded like the voice was coming from a million miles away, I knew who it was without having to look up. Miss Odessa. She lived at the other end of the projects but it goes to show you they were all there. That's how it was in the projects when something bad happened to somebody. It was always better to witness someone else's hard luck, the closer the better, rather than hear a second or third hand version later on. Being a witness could make people give you some respect, at least for as long as it took you to tell what you'd seen.

Miss Odessa put her hand on top of my head, so strong it felt like she was trying to push me into the ground. You want to talk about somebody big? Talk about Miss Odessa.

"Louis?"

I didn't answer. I only looked up because I could feel her pressing harder on my head and my knees were folding under me. I was trying to keep from sinking into the parking lot in front of the entire Stratfield Projects. I didn't want to look at her directly, so I stared instead at the Christmas corsage she had pinned to her coat with a huge gold safety pin. The corsage had white bells that looked like they were carved out of mothballs. I was focusing on the mothball bells when the cop asked me, "So what was the fight about?"

Trying to figure out how I was going to get out of saying anything to either Miss Odessa or him, I stared into the mouth of one of the bells and imagined sound coming out. Martha and the Vandellas again. *My arms keep missing you.* But now Miss Odessa was pushing even harder.

"Louis, the policeman's talking to you. Don't you hear the policeman talking to you?" The cop had his hand on my shoulder. The pressure from her was featherweight compared to the cop's grip.

First, I looked real hard at Miss Odessa to let her know even if she was pretending to be a friend of Mom's, I didn't believe it. I didn't like her and never had. Then I focused on the cop's face. I wanted to make sure he knew I was lying.

"I can't remember what the fight was about, sir. I can't remember anything."

And while both the cop and Miss Odessa kept pushing me down like trash in a can, they couldn't get me to say another word. I went over it in my mind, though. From the beginning. For myself. To make sure I really could remember it. It was important to keep all the details in some part of me that was safe, for later.

2

Ben had been in the bathroom with the door open for at least an hour, shaving and whistling in his suit pants and stocking cap. I was downstairs in the living room reading the Sunday comics, but I could look upstairs from my chair and see him. He always left the door open when he was shaving. And he always whistled when he shaved. He'd go through one song pretty simply, then start at the beginning again, doing a jazz version of the same thing, except this time he'd add a trill like opera singers do with their voices. So it was kind of a jazz-opera whistle.

Mom was in the kitchen banging the pots around and slamming the oven door. I couldn't tell if she was mad because she thought I should be upstairs doing homework instead of reading the comics, or if she was furious at Ben for something I hadn't heard about yet.

He was really showing off now, patting aftershave on his cheeks in time to the whistling. Lorelle stood at the foot of the stairs staring up at him, swaying, hypnotized by the same trills I rolled, then crossed my eyes at in disgust. Ben whistled himself into the bedroom, put on a shirt, tie, his suit jacket and the double-breasted black coat he kept in a fancy plastic cleaners bag and almost never wore.

The whole time he was shaving, dressing, patting and whistling, Mom threw silverware onto the table, piece by piece, each fork and knife harder and louder than the last.

Finally Ben came downstairs, jingling his car keys as another layer of accompaniment. Mom flew out of the kitchen. She had on a dark green dress dusted with white fingerprints all over it. She looked as though she'd dipped her hands in flour, then slapped herself from head to toe. There was flour in her hair, on her forehead, up and down her stockings. With her chest leading and her arms beating the air, she was a colored woman windmill spinning across the floor, spitting flour.

"Where are you going, mister?" she yelled into the space between his shoulders.

Ben kept walking toward the front door. He was doing a long, spiderleg stroll at an easy, good-time pace with Mom screaming at his back. He answered her, looking straight ahead like she was actually in front of him instead of behind.

"*I* am going to a Christmas party." He sounded cheerful, cocky, like he was about to add, "And I'm leaving *your* screaming butt here." Mom called him a Christmas party liar and asked him why the hell he didn't have the guts to say he was on his way to deliver his Christmas bonus to his woman. I always tried to picture this woman Mom was so sure Ben was going to. But there were never any real clues that I could put together.

He stopped at the door and looked over his shoulder to face her. He smiled as if he was looking at somebody who was going to disappear in a few minutes so it didn't matter what she said to him.

"Cause you already know that, don't you?" He turned around, opened the door and kept walking.

"Yeah, but what you don't know, mister bastard, is that I'm coming with you."

Mom ran past me to the hall closet. I jumped out of the

chair as though she'd yanked a rope tied around my neck. When she whizzed back by me again in the grizzly, following Ben out to the parking lot, I turned to Lorelle. With a look of terror in her eyes, she asked, "Louis, are you leaving me?"

"You stay here. I'll be right back." I ran after Mom. She was running now to keep up with Ben, even though he still didn't look like he was in much of a hurry. The grizzly looked like it was covered in powdered snow. Mom kept slipping on the ice yelling, "Christmas party, huh? Well, let's go!" But she didn't go down. I did.

By the time I got up, Ben had made it out to the parking lot, right up to the car. I thought, this will be the fight, because I knew he wouldn't let her get in with him. When he opened the door on his side, though, Mom pushed right past him. Ben stopped for a second—she'd surprised him—but then he got in too, closed the door and leaned over to start the engine.

I ran around to her side and pounded on the window. "Get out of the car, Mom. Get out."

She leaned over and opened her door. "Go back, Louis! Go back and stay with Lorelle!"

Instead, I got in the car, she moved to the middle and started beating on Ben. "Christmas party, huh!? Christmas party!?" with a punch for each one. Ben blocked her, grinning. "That's right. That's where I'm going." He grabbed both her arms so that all she could do was throw her whole body at him, kicking. I tried to pull her away, but there was too much of the grizzly for me to get a hold on her. Ben wouldn't let go. I reached past her and hit him myself.

Ben's grin disappeared. He held Mom off with one arm, and punched me square in the mouth, his high school ring knocking against my teeth. Now Mom went crazier, pulling herself free from him. Her fist thudded into his chest, his face, his chest again.

Ben's eyes popped wide like a jolt of electricity had gone through his body. His arms flopped to his sides. Mom stopped screaming. She looked at Ben, confused, as if in the six years they'd been married, she never remembered seeing him look exactly the way he did at that moment. We both watched him, waiting for him to move. It looked as if he was concentrating on how to steer the car out of the space it was in; like Mom and me had disappeared just that quickly and it was time for him to get on with driving to wherever he was going.

Then he made this noise as if he was pushing all the air out of his lungs. I watched his mouth. The color in his lips was fading, leaking out with the air. Till there wasn't any sound or color or air at all.

Mom whispered, "Je-sus." I think she knew then that he'd died, but I didn't. I never thought about him dying. I didn't think Ben *could* die.

When Isabelle Jackson ran up to the window, I realized how many people were standing around the car. Right away, I began to dream I could drive through all of them. Ben's green Pontiac with the bird shit splattered across the windows was lifting off at the end of the parking lot and ascending high above the projects, sailing out over the city.

I thought the cop might arrest me for not answering his questions. I knew I wasn't too young. Other kids had been hauled away in handcuffs. For stealing, mostly. But nobody, not even the worst ones, had killed anybody.

I stood there waiting in the cold between the cop and

Miss Odessa. She was making sure everybody would think she was an important part of what was going on. It probably looked to some people like she was helping the cop by not letting me get away, or to somebody else like maybe she was protecting me from him because my mother wasn't there.

Mom came back carrying Lorelle as the ambulance was leaving the parking lot with Ben. Lorelle looked more confused than she had when I'd left her. Mom never carried her anywhere. Lorelle was tall for her age and too heavy to be lifted, except in emergencies.

Nevertheless, Mom looked pretty calm, if a little winded, until she saw that Ben wasn't completely gone.

"Oh God, Ben! Oh God!" she called out to the back of the ambulance.

Miss Odessa ran over to her, but the sound Mom made then scared Miss Odessa so badly, she jumped back like she'd run over to a howling, killer dog. Mom continued half-calling, half-barking to Ben in the ambulance, although it was now completely out of view. The cops, the neighbors, no one took their eyes off her. Lorelle pulled away and stared, looking more curious than afraid. I studied Mom's eyes, the way she clamped her bottom teeth against her upper lip, how she clenched her fists around Lorelle's thighs so that the skin above and beneath her wedding ring looked pale and swollen around it. Nobody ever wanted to know what Mom would do next more than I did. But with Mom, I could never even begin to guess.

3

"This is for the funeral, Louis. What do you think?"

Gray, with padded shoulders and wide lapels, it looked very much like a man's suit, except there was a skirt to be worn under the jacket instead of pants. I particularly liked the contrast of the deeper gray, suede-covered buttons. I wondered where she got the money. What I asked instead was, "Why isn't it black?"

"I'm too old to wear black anymore," she said, "no matter what the occasion is. I put on black and look like somebody should be burying *me*." You weren't too old to wear it when you married him, I thought.

The year of her second wedding, Mom told me as she stood at the kitchen sink kneading hamburger meat, "I believe in the adventure of starting over. Sometimes you have to start over to get what you wanted from the beginning." Mom had brought me to Stratfield from New York when I was three with the intention of starting over. She had what she referred to as "*our* plan," meaning hers and mine, although in truth, it was like anything else she wanted us to do. She'd make a decision, then announce it as "*our* plan."

What she said she wanted, was to make sure I knew what it felt like to have a family. "I'm going to make us one," she told me. "You'll see. It won't be long. I can feel it." She took a handful of meat and slapped it emphatically into a pattie between her palms. "Until then, we have each other. And we have our apartment." Mom pronounced "apartment" as if she'd miraculously isolated our four rooms from the rest of the Stratfield Projects. What we had was one bedroom, a bathroom, a living room and a kitchen. The kitchen was small enough for the two of us to finish eating dinner at the table and put the dishes in the sink without getting up. We shared the bedroom, although Mom told me I was too big to be sleeping in the same bed with her. Whenever she got really angry with me, she'd sleep in the living room on the couch. I asked her if "*our* plan" included moving out of the projects to a real house or even a real apartment house like the ones in downtown Stratfield. They didn't have ripped screen doors or pitiful, stomped-on hedges in yards strewn with potato chip bags and cornflakes boxes.

"Of course, moving is part of *our* plan. You don't think *this* is the end of the road, do you? First, I have to make us a family. Then we'll move."

We couldn't move fast enough to suit me. As far as I was concerned, if living in the projects was part of the plan, Mom had already made a big mistake. One of my first memories of living there was the afternoon of my sixth birthday. Mom and I had celebrated with our own party. I didn't know or like any of the project kids well enough to invite them into our apartment. A few of them had taken turns shoving me around since we'd moved in. Nothing too serious, but not exactly "let's be best friends" either. Usually, I ventured out only when I'd checked beforehand to see if the courtyard was empty. At the first sign of another kid, I disappeared inside. It seemed to me to be the safest way to deal with it until I could come up with a better strategy.

When Mom asked me if I was sure I wanted it to be only the two of us for my party, I said I was, insisting though that we still get dressed up. I chose my navy blue velvet jacket with the matching tie. She wore pearls with a camel-colored sweater set and alligator shoes. Toasting me with cream soda in a stemmed wine glass, she kissed me and whispered, "To Louis, on the day made just for him." The two of us had such a fine time that I drifted quite contentedly outside to sit on the stoop and read from my favorite present, an illustrated edition of *Grimm's Fairy-Tales* with gold-edged pages. I'd already read "The Fisherman and His Wife" several times, fascinated by the pictures of the fisherman on his knees at the ocean. And I stared into the pinched face of his dissatisfied wife, shaking her fist at the sky.

Bubba Graves came across the courtyard and up to the stoop. "Sissy, who you think you are?"

The afternoon had left me feeling pretty bold. "Go away, onionhead," I told Bubba who was eight and at least a foot taller than me. He reached over and pulled me up by the collar of my jacket. "Who you callin' onionhead?"

"You see anybody else around here with a head like yours?" I replied, struggling to get away.

Bubba looked furious at first. Then he started to fake a laugh. He pulled the jacket off me and threw it to the ground. Standing on it, he grabbed one sleeve and pulled on it grunting and dribbling, his eyes crossing and uncrossing again. When I heard it rip, I screamed like he'd torn my arm from its socket. He waved the sleeve in the air above my head shouting, "Look at your sissy jacket now! I fixed it for ya!" I stumbled into the house, holding the ruined jacket to my chest.

Mom ran downstairs and stormed over to the Graveses' apartment. When she held the jacket up in front of Inez

24

Graves, demanding to know what she intended to do about it, Bubba's mother barked at her, "That's what the hell you get for sending your boy outside looking like a little white girl."

Mom was a department manager at Saks Fifth Avenue in downtown Stratfield. She'd worked for Saks in New York City before she moved to Connecticut. Proud of being a department manager, she told me there weren't any other black women managers in the New York or the Stratfield store.

From the time I started school, I stayed at Miss Odessa's until Mom picked me up on her way home from Saks. Miss Odessa asked me everything about Mom she didn't dare ask her, knowing Mom would tell her it was none of her business. Being a kid, I couldn't say anything like that to Miss Odessa so I usually pretended I didn't understand what she was asking. I'd wait until Mom picked me up to tell her in front of Miss Odessa, "Mom, Miss Odessa wants to know how much you get paid to get dressed up and walk around Saks all day with a badge on, but I told her she should ask you." Miss Odessa would be pretty snitty with me for the next few days when we were alone, but it was worth it.

Every once in a while Mom would bring a guy home and we'd put on a kind of show for him. She'd cook and then go change into one of her dresses that she said was from the New York days. While she was changing, I was supposed to read to the guy from whatever book I'd taken out of the library. She'd make me read because it was pretty much the only way she could get me to talk in front of him and because it also made me seem as smart as she'd told him I was. The few nights I tried to make some excuse for not reading, like not having a library book that week, she'd wait until the guy left and wake me up to let me have it.

"I don't care if you read him the telephone bill. You do what I ask you to do when I ask you to do it. Don't try to make a liar out of me, Louis." It took me a while to figure out that these nights were her sales presentations and the sales presentations were part of "*our* plan." If I didn't do my part, it made it harder for her to sell both of us to the guy.

The night she brought Ben home, I knew it was important. Some of the others had been a lot better looking or friendlier. A couple of them, I could tell, would have liked both of us, whether I could read or not. Most of them, once she'd changed into the New York dress, didn't really listen to what I was reading. They just wanted me to hurry up and go to bed or anywhere so they could be alone with her. But with this Ben guy, she was nervous.

"Ben works in the shipping department," she said when she introduced him, "as an order clerk. Of course, a man as smart as Ben should be a manager. But they wouldn't make a black *man* a manager for anything."

She didn't act like she was having fun at all, but she was definitely working hard. When she changed into the New York dress he didn't seem to notice, and I could tell she was disappointed. I felt sorry for her, so I tried to do my part better than usual. There's only so much I could do with a library book except to read really loudly and exaggerate the different characters' voices like I was playing all the parts in a movie. I thought it was going pretty well, especially the narration, which I was reading with a deep Southern drawl to make it more interesting. I looked up about halfway through and Ben was staring at me as if maybe he was a little afraid of me, even if I was only eight.

Mom looked like she was in shock, like she couldn't understand what I was doing, but didn't know how to stop it. Later, after he left, when she got into bed I pretended to be asleep but she knew I wasn't. "I just want you to ask me for something," she said in the dark, turned away from me. "I'm just waiting for you to ask me for something you really want."

Two nights later, when we were having dinner, Mom told me, "Ben says you're definitely too old to be sleeping in the same bed with me."

I excused myself and pushed away from the table so I wouldn't have to look at her. I got this picture of Ben stealing into our room in the middle of the night, staring at us, then shaking his head and sneaking back out of the apartment. What did it matter to him where I slept? Why was she talking about it with him?

"We're all going out Saturday night. Make sure you have a nice, clean shirt and pants to wear."

I stopped and turned back to her. "All of us?" I don't know why I asked. I'd heard her alright. Maybe I hoped I had a choice.

At the Chinese restaurant, Ben ordered everything for us without asking us what we wanted, pretending to read Chinese from the menu like he knew what he was doing. Mom started to laugh.

"Ben speaks French, too."

But when Ben looked at her as if he wasn't sure if she was making fun of him, she said, "So does Louis, Ben. Maybe you can talk to each other in French. Go ahead, Louis. Say something to Ben in French."

"I don't really speak French," I said to Ben quietly. "My class had a substitute last year who was Canadian. She taught us 'bonjour,' 'merci' and 'comment allez-vous,' but that's all I know."

"Well, that's French, isn't it?" Mom asked me, in a huff. "Why did you contradict me, Louis?" Then she gave Ben her wide smile again. "Ben, you say something to Louis in French."

Ben looked down into his empty plate, up again at her and finally at me. He shrugged. "Bonjour" and "merci" and uh, the other one, huh? Well, I guess you got one on me, then. I'm strictly a hello and thank-you kinda guy."

"I certainly don't know any other black men who can speak a foreign language at all," Mom said quickly. "And I've got two right here at this table."

I watched them, saying as little as possible after that. When we got home I got yelled at for being rude, which surprised me since I'd been careful to call Ben Mr. Ben. I'd said, "Please, Mr. Ben," "Thank you, Mr. Ben," and "No, thank you, Mr. Ben." I decided it was something else he'd told her, and I was beginning to understand that what he said was important to her, whether it was true or not.

For the next few weeks, I knew Mom was still dating Ben, but we didn't talk about him at all. First on Saturday nights, then on Friday nights as well, I packed my books and pajamas and went to Miss Odessa's. I only saw Ben when they both came to pick me up. Mom always asked me if I wanted to stay at Miss Odessa's until morning and I always said no. Ben would walk us through the projects back to our apartment in the middle of the night. He never said anything to me, but I heard him tell Mom one night that she should just tell me what to do, that where I slept should be her choice not mine.

One Friday, before they went out, she told me to sit on the couch so she could talk to me. I knew trouble was coming. Mom never told me where to sit before she said something. Ben went to the bedroom door and inspected our room as if he was deciding whether Mom and I kept it neat or not. Mom said, "Louis, Ben and I are going to get married."

She said even though the wedding hadn't happened yet they were thinking I could call him Daddy Ben or just Dad now if I wanted. "Which one do you think, hon?" I sat watching Ben, who still had his back to both of us, staring into the bedroom.

"Why can't I just keep calling him Mr. Ben?" I asked her. I don't know whether I really said it so quietly or if she was stalling for time to think of what to say. "Ben, did you hear Louis? He asked me why he couldn't just keep calling you Mr. Ben. I don't know how to answer that, Ben."

Ben turned from looking into the bedroom and walked over to where I was sitting on the couch.

"Flip. He's being flip. Because you let him get away with it."

Ben stood over me. "Let me tell you something, Louis. From what your mother says, there are snot-noses out there a helluva lot smaller than you are taking pot shots at you. Maybe it's because of your smart-aleck mouth. But you know what, buddy? You've met your match with me. Now try this on for size. You can call me Mr. Ben if you want to. But only if you call your mother Mrs. Ben from now on, too. Okay? Now what do you have to say about that, Mr. Flip?" I looked down at my shoes, hoping Mom and Ben had to leave soon and this part would be over.

The next morning, Mom sat on my side of the bed and said gently, "Could you try calling him Daddy Ben just to see how you like it? It'll be better for all of us. You'll see."

Two weeks later, she showed me a very plain, black dress with long tight sleeves that she said she'd bought to get married in. "This is about the finest silk there is," she said proudly. "Feel it." I ran my fingers around the collar. I hadn't expected it to be black. She looked beautiful in it, though, standing next to Ben in our living room. They stood facing the minister from the church me and Mom went to, with their backs to me, Miss Odessa and Miss Odessa's boyfriend, Albert. The three of us sat on the couch because there wasn't room in the living room for all of us to stand. When the ceremony was over, the adults drank champagne and Mom gave me a glass of ginger ale. With each sip, I pretended I was getting drunker. I went into the bathroom and spun around in circles until I got dizzy. Then I sat on the toilet, and rasped in my drunk voice the same thing Miss Odessa kept saying to Mom, "Jeanette, you got him, girl! You got him now!"

I must have been in there for a long time, because Mom knocked on the door to ask if I was alright. When I went back out to the living room, Miss Odessa and her boyfriend were gone and I didn't see Ben either. Mom was sitting at one end of the couch. It had been made up like a bed, the way it was when I stayed home sick and she let me come out and watch television or when she was angry with me and slept out there herself.

From where I stood, I could see Ben in the bedroom, in his undershirt, taking off his watch. I thought at that moment he was probably the tallest man I'd ever seen, a giant in a dollhouse. I looked back to the couch. My pajamas were folded, placed in the middle of my pillow like they were a present. I couldn't look at Mom. She reached for me and I stood there as she hugged me, kissed me on my forehead, my nose, then both sides of my face.

"Good night, baby."

I wasn't going to answer, but I knew she wouldn't go away if I didn't.

"Night."

I bent down to take off my shoes. She started toward the bedroom, then turned when she got to the door.

"Did you say good night to Daddy Ben?"

I hung my pants over the chair, leg to leg, ankle to ankle.

"Good night, Daddy Ben."

I hoped it was loud enough. I didn't want to have to say it again.

"Good night."

The door was already closed.

On Saturdays, Ben left for work at seven-thirty. I pretended to be asleep until eight. If I stayed in bed any later, Mom threw up every shade, slammed every drawer and dragged all the furniture around like she was single-handedly moving us to another apartment. By then, I was up and scurrying, trying to make up for lost time.

It was all Mom's furniture that she'd bought from Saks. I thought Ben would've brought something with him besides his clothes, but Mom said he'd been living in a furnished room. "It's just as well," she'd told me, "I haven't met anybody in this town with the same taste as I have. I can't imagine what I'd do if I had to cram a lot of junk in here that I couldn't stand looking at."

As soon as I dressed and ate, we scrubbed and waxed together. We crawled through the apartment on our knees, with sponges, rags, steel wool pads, buckets of boiled water and ammonia. Around noon, depending on how much we'd finished, Mom sent me to Big Lou's to buy a half pound of lunch meat, two fresh hard rolls, a pack of Salem cigarettes, a bottle of ginger ale and a half pint of scotch. In the beginning, Mom would call the liquor store before I got there, or send a note with me. But after a while, the man didn't even look at the note and eventually I told Mom I didn't need one anymore.

When I got back to the apartment, she'd still be on her knees in a corner. "You get everything, alright?"

I'd unpack it all and lay it out on the kitchen table. Mom came in and opened the cigarettes first. She'd stick out her lips and push the cigarette in between them to taste it, run her tongue over it. With a single hard pop of the match, she'd light it. The first drag was slow and long. She held the smoke, then let it drift out between her lips slowly without moving. Then, she'd reach for a small paring knife to break the seal on the scotch. "Get a couple of glasses down."

With her first sip, she scrunched up her nose as if she didn't like the way it smelled. After the next, more swallow than sip, she'd go into the living room and put on a record. Sometimes Billie Holiday, sometimes Dinah Washington. She'd sing the first line of the song with them before she came back into the kitchen.

"You want a little ginger ale?"

I always imagined it was scotch. She'd add a little soda to her drink. "Come on and sing with me, baby."

Most of the time, if she was in a good mood, good enough to ask me to sing with her, it meant the afternoon would be filled with music and stories, mostly funny, of growing up in Harlem, New York. Sometimes, though, the stories weren't funny, and her mood changed like the records she played. Suddenly she was angry, talking to herself as though I wasn't there.

"From sugar to shit," she'd say and shrug, scraping a spot on the linoleum with her knife. "Right now, I got about a tenth of what I started out with." She'd pour another scotch, without the ginger ale.

When I was nine, she stopped one Saturday morning in the middle of a drink and looked at me hard, as though she hadn't noticed me before sitting in front of her.

"That. That thing you're doing now. That's why Ben says you're a damn punk. He says he can tell already you're gonna be a faggot. I'd appreciate it if you proved him wrong."

I froze, barely breathing, trying not to do anything. Mom had started to perspire a little, the muscles in her neck more pronounced, like thick rubber tubes balancing her head. She was through singing with Dinah. The good part of Saturday was over.

4

"You're about to cheap your life away, Ben Stamps. People have to eat. If it were up to you," she told him, "we'd be growing our own food in the projects courtyard."

Thursday night meant Grand Union. I hated grocery shopping because it was boring and because Ben and Mom fought every week about how much money to spend. Ben said we were spoiled because Mom had bought anything she wanted when it was just the two of us, but now it was his money too and she had to learn how to budget.

Usually, he waited in the parking lot while Mom and I shopped. When we came out, he'd drive up in front of the store and wait in the car while Mom and I put the packages in the trunk. After we'd finished, Mom and I would get in, she'd count out the change, and he'd start an argument about how half of what she'd just bought was unnecessary.

One night, after I'd jumped in the back, Mom slammed herself in and exploded. "Any other man with a pregnant wife would get off his behind and help me with those heavy bags. But you, you're in here whistling and waiting, ready to chew me out about paying too damn much for butter and milk."

I was stunned. Mom hadn't told me she was pregnant. She didn't look any different to me. I waited until our Saturday morning together to ask her about it.

"Yep," she said casually, apparently not hearing the

frustration in my voice at being left out of a development that would surely change everything. "What do you want, sister or brother? Ben doesn't seem to care one way or the other and I'll be happy as long as the baby's healthy—fingers, toes, and everything else where it's supposed to be. So it's up to you. What'll it be?"

"I don't know," I answered. "I never thought about it." At that moment, I was more concerned about where we'd all live. For the past year, the three of us had shared Mom's one bedroom apartment. I was beginning to think it would always be like that. Or at least, until I was old enough to move out.

Mom said the new baby was the reason we'd be able to move to some place with more room. I thought she was talking about a house like the ones across the street from the projects, but we weren't leaving the projects. We were moving to what the projects management called a bungalow. It had two floors so it seemed like a house, but all the bungalows were attached, which meant you could still hear the people next door pee and flush the toilet. The good part was that I'd finally have my own room, which to me sounded like being able to escape to another country. There'd be a separate room for the baby, too. With three bedrooms and a bathroom upstairs and the kitchen and the living room downstairs, there'd be a lot more to clean than before.

Mom hired two men she knew from Saks to help us move, without telling Ben, which made him furious. She said she had no choice since no one in the projects would lift a finger to help us. She was right. People came out onto their stoops to watch us carry boxes across the courtyard, but no one offered to take one. Mom said to me, "You see how jealous they are. That's because they know our next move will be *out* of this damn jungle and they'll be here for the rest of their lives."

She was still working at Saks, but she also found another job cleaning offices at night. "We need more money now that the baby is coming," she told me. "Ben's already upset at how much more rent we'll have to pay now. I'm trying to meet him halfway with it. At least, while I still can." When I asked her about looking more tired than I'd ever seen her, she said, "It's only a little longer. Babies cost money. And I'm not scrimping on anything, no matter what Ben says."

In order to save, she stopped making appointments to have her hair done. Instead, she sat in front of the stove and pulled the smoking hot comb through her tight, wooly cap of hair until it was all standing away from her face like an Indian headdress. Before, when she'd come back from Miss Helen's Beauty Box, she had a garden of perfect, black shiny curls in even rows all around her head. Now, she curled only the front herself. She said as she got bigger that it was too hard to reach the back. "Besides," she said, "I'm doing a good enough job burning up the front."

She made maternity clothes on the sewing machine she'd brought from New York. Big dresses, big blouses, big skirts. All in solid colors. Lots of different blues or greens, but no polka dots like the white women on the pattern covers.

"Pregnant or no pregnant, I'm not interested in looking like Lucy Ricardo," Mom said. "No polka dots for me, thank you."

Ben came home from work one night and handed Mom a soiled brown grocery bag. He told her Shirley Green, a woman with seven kids who lived in the 4C building, had called to him on his way in from the parking lot. She'd dropped the bag from her upstairs window and yelled down for him to deliver it to Mom. Mom told Ben to go ahead and sit down to the table to eat. She stood by the stove holding the bag away from her as if she suspected there was something crawling around inside it, waiting for a chance to escape. After Ben and I began to eat, Mom slowly opened the bag and pulled out two wrinkled, dingy maternity blouses. She unfolded them, held each of them up to the light, examining the collars and the underarms. Refolding them, she put them back into the bag. Then, she went to the sink and washed her hands, splattering water everywhere.

Ben spoke without looking up from his plate. "Of course, it makes more sense to you to spend money buying fancy material to make clothes than to stoop so low as to wear something that somebody gives you. Somebody who used to know you from New York might pass through the projects and recognize you in a dress that wasn't from Saks."

Mom reached down and raised the bag up again under the bare lightbulb in our yellow kitchen. "Somebody pass a law saying I have to wear somebody's stinking handmedown clothes just cause I'm living in the city's stinking handmedown apartment? Tell Shirley Green I said, 'No, thank you. I'll do fine with what I have.'"

Ben kept eating like he hadn't heard her. Mom never sat down at all. She cleaned around and around the pots on the top of the stove, down its front and sides. Then she started on the top again. When Ben's plate was empty, he got up, placed it in the sink with barely a sound and went into the living room. Ben hardly made any noise ever, doing anything. Even when he spoke, his voice was lower and softer than either Mom's or mine. When they argued, the louder Mom's voice got, the quieter his was, which seemed to make her even angrier. Unless you listened well, all you could hear was her, which made her sound like she was crazy, screaming for no reason at all. Ben never sounded like he was arguing. He sounded like he was explaining the truth to someone who didn't understand it. But his voice was his weapon and when he used it on her, she shouted as though he'd hit her.

Late that night when they started, I got up and went to my door. Ben asked her like it was a word problem in math he wanted her to solve. If she was so much better than everybody in the projects, what was she doing living there when he met her?

"Doing a whole lot better than I'm doing now." She repeated it over and over again, pacing back and forth across the floor of their bedroom. I got back in bed and put my pillow over my head, but I could still hear her. "A whole lot better than I'm doing now." I fell asleep trying to remember what she'd looked like then, when she was doing a whole lot better.

When my sister Lorelle was born, I can't say Mom looked like she had before she met Ben, but it was definitely an improvement. She would stay home now, she said, at least until Lorelle went to school. "God, do I miss the store, Louis," she'd confide to me about Saks. "I'll probably go back part-time when the baby's a little older." But about the night job she said, "I sure as hell don't miss scrubbing down a hundred desk chairs." She looked like she was pleased with herself and the baby, as if she'd set out to prove something and won. We still had our Saturdays together. She never stopped telling me stories about Birdland, Sugar Hill, the old Apollo. If she'd had more than two scotches, she'd start to talk about her old boyfriends and by late afternoon, she began to talk about Louis, her first Louis. She never called him my father. That wasn't the important part. The important part was that Louis was part of her good times, the times before now. What she wouldn't say, no matter how many scotches she'd had, was what what I wanted to know most. Why wasn't the Louis she'd wanted to remember so badly she'd given me his name, why wasn't this Louis ever coming home? Where had he disappeared to?

It was her first Louis, she said, who'd made sure she got to meet Billie Holiday. "He knew Billie would want one of my dresses, one of Jeanette's Originals. I wasn't working from any store-bought patterns then. I had my own designs. A lot of people sewed, but there were only three black women in Harlem who'd made the kind of name for themselves I had. I had the clients the other two couldn't get, from doctors' wives to Cotton Club showgirls." She lit another cigarette and poured more scotch into her glass. "You want a little soda?"

"Yes," I mumbled. But I wanted scotch. I wanted to feel the same things she was feeling, in the same way she felt them. Through old records and cigarette smoke.

"From the time I met Louis, he said that's all I ever talked about. Seeing Billie onstage singing in a Jeanette Original. So he said he figured he didn't have any choice but to make sure it happened. That's the way he talked."

"And he did make sure it happened, right?"

"Yeah. Cause that's what he was. Half con man, half magician. One minute he'd make a dream come true, next minute he'd open his hands and it would all be gone."

"But what about Billie?" I wanted to know. Had he made good on his promise to her about Billie?

"One night, he takes me to this club where she's playing on Fifty-seventh Street. This guy he knows who works there is showing us to a table and Louis leans over to me and whispers, 'After the set, you're going back to meet Billie. We're gonna make you famous. Tonight!'

"Well, I didn't have any sketches of my work or photographs or anything with me. So I wasn't feeling real grateful at first. Me and Louis started going back and forth at each other." Mom stopped. She smiled, but not at me. With her legs crossed and a cigarette held up in the air, she was posing as if somebody'd been taking her picture the whole time she was supposed to be telling me her story. This was her interview, for magazine or newspaper, it probably didn't matter, really. The important thing was she felt she deserved an audience of more than just me. For her, somebody else was in the room listening, taking it all down, so that it was as much history as any headline in the *Daily News*. Now I knew, but it still somehow felt private. I felt lucky she let me be there to hear it.

"Louis tore out of there. Jumped in a cab. Went home and got the photo album I'd put together showing half the women on Sugar Hill in my clothes. He was back before Billie even got onstage.

"After she finished, we had to to go around to the side entrance and wait for somebody to show me to her dressing room. I don't know whether she knew I was waiting or not, but we stood out there in that alley for a half hour. I was so nervous, I went through my album three times, down on my hands and knees changing the pictures around in the dark.

"Billie had on a white satin robe like a prizefighter's

with makeup all over it. She said, 'So you're a dress-maker.' I told her no, I was a designer. She laughed and said, 'Hell, and I'm a jazz artist,' real sarcastic. I was ready to leave then, without showing her my damn book, but she told me, 'Take it easy, baby. I'm just trying to keep it light.' She said she wanted to show me something a woman had made for her and ask me what I thought of it. She brought out a red one-shouldered gown with painted seashells glued in big circles on it and a split up the front.

"What kinda trip you think this bitch is on?' Billie asked me. Cause you know ain't no way in hell I'll be wearin' this bad joke anywhere.' "

Mom told me she made two dresses for Billie. "You want to see the pictures?" Yes, of course, I wanted to see the pictures. I wanted to see them all.

"I'm gonna dig them out for you. I will. Right after I feed Lorelle."

But after she made lunch for Lorelle, somehow it was too late. The spell cast over the kitchen was gone. The interview was over. I'd have to wait for her to give another so I could ask her again about Billie and how she'd almost been famous.

5

Sixth grade. Social Studies. Joseph Monolucci stumbles through the end of the chapter called "Alaska and Its People: The Eskimos." I've already turned the page to go over the words of the new chapter in case I'm called on to read. I'm the best in class at reading out loud. Even though mine is supposed to be the smartest sixth-grade class in the school, there are kids who have trouble with any words having more than two syllables. Or else they just read so slowly, Miss Murphy lets them get through a paragraph, says "Good," and then calls on somebody else.

The new chapter is called "Africa and Its People: From Watusi to Pygmy." My stomach knots when I see the black-and-white photographs of people who are practically naked, except for what look like rags tied around them. The photograph makes their skin look so dark it would be hard to make out their features if they weren't all smiling. One picture is of three men who are taller and thinner than any man I've ever seen, black or white. There's a photograph next to it of a white man, a woman and a child, all fully dressed. The little boy has on a Yankees baseball cap. Under the picture of the three tall black men it says, "Three African Watusis" and under the white people it says, "Average American Family." The white man in the Average American Family picture comes up to the waist of the men in the Watusi photograph.

On the opposite page, there's another picture of about

ten or twelve black people who look like small children, except for four of them who have old faces. They are all smiling. Everyone in all of the pictures is smiling, except the Africans are showing their teeth and the Average American Family is smiling with their mouths closed. Under the picture of the black people who look like small children it says "Pygmy Family." All the members of the Pygmy family are wearing diapers.

I'm still staring at the pictures, not paying attention to where the class is in the reading at all. I hear the word "Africa" a lot, so I know we haven't finished the chapter. Miss Murphy is calling on me to read. She's calling me Louie, which isn't my name, but I've told her that a couple of times since the beginning of the term. Mom says white people always do that with a black person's name, change it to something that sounds like nobody could take the person seriously. She asked me if I wanted her to come in and straighten Miss Murphy out, but I said no. She'd said something to Mr. D'Estephano at Parents' Night last year about doing the same thing. The next morning he kept saying, "Louisss," and hissing the s so loud, the other kids started to do it and it took a week before it stopped.

"Louie, are you daydreaming over there?"

Somebody giggles in the corner.

"No, Miss Murphy," I answer. I look over at Peter Anatello to make sure I have the right page, but he moves his book so I can't see it.

"We're on page one-seventy-nine, Louie," she says in a very low voice, talking between her teeth. "Right under the picture of the pygmies."

I clear my throat, knowing I better make it a good reading. But Miss Murphy has started to laugh, so now I'm confused about whether she still wants me to read or not.

"Do you know why I'm laughing, class?" We're all looking at her, but it doesn't seem like anybody can guess the answer.

"I'm laughing because I was thinking how much you look like one of these little people here, Louie. One of these little pygmies."

She barely gets it out before the whole class is shouting with laughter. Laughing like they did when she went out of the room, Mary Beth Savarrici went into the coatroom to get her lunch and David Pacerella locked her in. Or when Joseph Monolucci pulled the chair out from under Anita Collabella and the desk turned over on her, too. Laughing so loud Miss Murphy has to tell them to quiet down, not like she's mad but like she doesn't want anyone else to hear. Then she says, still smiling herself, "Did you figure out where we are yet, Louie?"

"Yes, Miss Murphy. I know where we are." Even though I clear my throat, it comes out a whisper. I start to read and for the first time I'm not listening to myself. I'm just reading fast, hoping she'll call somebody else's name soon. By the time she does, it feels like I've been reading for about two hours.

I'm not sure whether I'm going to tell Mom about Miss Murphy saying I look like a pygmy or not. I know it would mean she'll be in the principal's office tomorrow for sure and then the whole school would know. It would only make it worse, like last year with Mr. D'Estephano.

But by the time the end of the day comes, the whole school knows anyway because about fifteen kids start chanting, "Louie, Louie, the pygmy, pygmy!" when I come out of the building. I know I'm supposed to punch at least one of them or as many as I can, but the last thing I want is to get beat up in front of everybody on top of everything else. There are about five boys I can see from where I'm standing who already call me Little Whitey because I'm the only black kid in my class. I can't risk the pygmy story getting any bigger than it already is so I just keep walking toward home.

Mom has this way of seeing on my face if something is wrong and pushing me to tell her until I do. I don't even get to the part about the kids outside school, which by now feels to me like the worst part. All she hears is the part about Miss Murphy saying I look like a pygmy and she's not listening anymore. She's on the phone, asking to speak to Mr. Kilgallen, the principal, and speaking in this voice that she always uses when she speaks to white people. The only white people she doesn't use it on are the ones in the projects. The school secretary tells Mom Mr. Kilgallen has already left the building. For Mom, that only means tomorrow can't come fast enough.

The next day she sends me to school at the regular time because she says she doesn't want to embarass me by going with me. Instead, she leaves the apartment a minute after I do and follows me. I barely get to my classroom before I get called to Mr. Kilgallen's office, where Mom is waiting with her head tilted so far up she looks like she has on an invisible neck brace. Mr. Kilgallen makes me repeat what Miss Murphy said about me looking like a pygmy.

After I do, Mom asks him, "Are you going to fire her now, or should I leave here and go directly to the Board of Education?"

I don't hear what Mr. Kilgallen answers myself, because he tells me to go back to class then, but by the time I get home, Mom has called the Board of Education anyway.

Miss Murphy didn't get fired. But I could tell how mad she was from the way she treated me in class for the next two days. Then we all met in Mr. Kilgallen's office again and Miss Murphy apologized to both me and Mom with this face that looked like she had a rubber mask on.

Mr. Kilgallen asked Mom if she wanted me taken out of Miss Murphy's class. "You know that means he'd be put in a lower group, don't you?" which meant I wouldn't be in the smart group anymore. Mom didn't even look at me before she answered. "Why would I punish my son because you hired a Nazi to teach him?" She stared at Miss Murphy and told him, "If she makes any more comparisons to pygmies, I'm going to my congressman. And as of this minute, I want her to begin calling my son by the name *I* gave him." Mr. Kilgallen sort of laughed and hiccupped at the same time. Miss Murphy said she was sorry again if Mom was offended and asked if she could be excused.

"Mrs. Stamps," Mr. Kilgallen said to Mom, "you certainly do get yourself worked up."

When I got home, Mom and I went over the story about sixty times, taking turns playing Mr. Kilgallen and Miss Murphy. Lorelle laughed along as if she understood perfectly what the performance was about. Mostly Mom kept telling me to play *her,* but every time I did she'd say, "Oh, I never said that. That's not real. You're making it up." And it probably did sound made up by then, even to her. Often, when I described something Mom said or did, it seemed made up. But if you'd been a part of it, if you were anywhere around it, you knew how real it was.

6

When I first saw Jackie Wilson on *Saturday Hit Parade,* I was in seventh grade. Mom heard him singing from the kitchen and asked me, "Who's singing like that, Louis?"

"A new guy named Jackie Wilson," I called back. "He's black." Before he'd come on, I'd been dancing around with Lorelle in my arms, but I put her down now, unable to do anything but stare at the television screen. Jackie Wilson was the prettiest black man I'd ever seen, with high, jutting cheekbones and skin that looked like powdered satin. He was also one of the few black men I'd seen on *Hit Parade.* There were groups sometimes where nobody particularly stood out, but not that many solo acts. No one like this.

"Nothing new about Jackie Wilson. He's just new to you. This must be his comeback," she said. "Some woman shot him up good a few years ago. He almost died. I'm surprised he can talk, much less sing."

Somebody shot him?! Now I had to get down on my knees, closer to the screen. I turned the volume up. Jackie Wilson sang higher than any man I'd ever heard and wore a suit with pants so tight you could see his calf muscles. He'd take off his tie, then his jacket, singing the whole time, and you could see how much he was sweating. Shirt soaked through, his chest and stomach smooth and dark under his white dress shirt. He jerked his head from side to side until his long processed hair fell over his forehead. He looked dangerous.

The song was a warning to somebody they better stop messing around, Jackie's heart was breaking and he didn't know how much longer he'd be able to take the pain. He was holding the microphone as if this was the person he was singing to, with his big, ringed fingers wrapped around their face and neck. He wanted to kiss them, but they'd hurt him so much, he might have to hurt them back. "You'd bettah stop, baby, messin', messin' round," he moaned, his voice swooping from a trembling soprano to a hoarse, rusty shout. He fell to his knees cradling the microphone one moment, looking like he was strangling it the next.

Love. And danger. On his knees, sweating and screaming with his hair hanging. "You bet-tah stop, baby, messin', messin' round." I wanted him to scream about me like that.

When *Hit Parade* was over, Mom started upstairs. "Bring Lorelle, Louis," she instructed. When I looked into their bedroom, she was leaning into her mirror, trying to even out the black hills she'd drawn for eyebrows. "Come in here. I want to talk to you about Christmas."

I went in and sat on the side of the bed where Ben slept. Leaning over onto his pillow, I imagined his face under my elbow.

"Do you realize you have to be the only thirteen-year-old in the world who can't ride a damn bicycle?"

This wasn't the first time she'd asked me if I realized everyone around me could ride a bike. What I wanted to know was, why did it matter so much to her?

"There isn't a child out there who can't ride a bike unless they're blind or crippled. Every year I ask you if you want one and you say no. This year I made up my mind I'm going to get you one and you'll learn to ride it."

Other kids in the projects had bikes, but no one had one

that was new. Sure, the older guys rode new bikes, but they were stolen and everybody knew because they bragged about it to anybody who'd listen. A new bike would probably get me killed.

Christmas morning, I knew I was looking at trouble. The first thing I thought when I saw it was that it looked like a brand-new red lipstick with tires. If there was anywhere in the world I could've gotten away with a bike like this, it wasn't the Stratfield Projects.

Right after dinner she told me, "You can take the bike out now. Remember, they say the only way to learn how to ride is to stay on it."

"What about the ice? I shouldn't take it out on the ice, should I?"

"There's not that much ice out there. I'll bet if any other kid in the projects got one, they'd be out there, ice or no ice. Learn now. It'll be spring before you know it."

I walked the bike around and around the courtyard, trying to get up the courage to jump the pedal closest to me with one foot and throw my other leg over the bar to the other side. If I could just get on it, pushing the pedals to keep it going couldn't be that hard. When I did push off on my side, I couldn't get my leg up and over to the other side fast enough before the bike fell over onto the ice. I jumped up, looking down to the other end for Mom, just in case. I tried a few more times. Each time, the bike crashed to the ground. Finally, I looked up and there she was, coming toward me in her coat and bedroom slippers.

"What's going on out here? Can you ride it yet?"

"No, ma'am. Not yet," I told her.

"Well, I want to see you ride it today. I asked Ben to come out here to help you."

"No. Please. I don't need him." A lesson from Ben was the last thing I wanted. I could feel eyes on me from all over the projects. It was only a matter of time before I'd be surrounded.

"What's the matter with you? Maybe if you gave him a chance every once in a while, the two of you could be friends."

I felt trapped in a world like those glass snow scenes with the miniature houses and all the water sloshing from side to side. I would have given anything to be able to disappear through a crack in the ice, leaving the bike to whoever wanted it.

Mom went inside and in moments Ben came out in a jacket, galoshes, and one of those hats with the bib and flaps. It wasn't that cold, but I guessed he thought he'd be out there for a while.

"Your mother seems to think you need help out here."

"Yes, sir."

"Well, this is usually something kids teach themselves. If it was something you wanted to do, I'm sure you'd find a way to learn it. You being as smart as you are." He held the back of the seat and nodded for me to start.

I ran, pushed down hard on the pedal closest to me with my outside leg, and threw my leg up and over to the other side. Ben continued to hold on to the seat, running behind me. I pumped as hard and as fast as I could, especially after he let go. For a moment I thought there'd been a miracle. I seemed to be suspended, held up by invisible strings as the bike sped forward. When I got to the corner, I panicked. I turned the handlebars sharply, feeling the bike quiver beneath me. I'd lost control. I crashed, noisily.

In these few minutes, as I expected, several boys had

gathered in the courtyard. At first, they stood in the distance snickering. Ben said nothing as we repeated the sequence. Pedal, pedal, fall. Pedal, pedal, crash. Each time, the snickers got louder. Each time, I glanced at Ben, hoping he'd decide on some way to end the whole thing.

Finally, as I scrambled to get up from what I'd decided was the absolutely last fall I'd let any one of them witness, they surrounded Ben and me yelling, "Why don't ya let me ride? C'mon, let me ride it!"

Ben started to grin at them. "Hold on," he said. "Hold on, guys." I stared at him, waiting to see how he was going to get rid of them.

He stood in front of them, like he was going to try to reason with them. "Who here knows how to ride?" he asked.

They all began yelling, "I do!" "I *been* knowin' how to ride!" "Please, please let me ride it, please!"

If this was a plan to distract them, I thought, Ben was wrong. They'd never give up now.

"Come on," he invited the closest, whose name I didn't even know. "Just a short one, though."

I stood watching as they took turns, fighting over who would go next.

No one spoke to me, not Ben, not any of them. I was shaking with anger, but I couldn't look at him. Mom had to be watching. She had to know what she'd started.

When the last boy had taken his ride around the courtyard, Ben turned to me and asked, "Well, did you learn something by watching at least?"

"Yes, sir," I said evenly, looking past him toward the apartment.

"You want to try again?"

"No, sir." I took the handlebars and slowly walked the

bike home. I knew Ben was following me. I could hear the boys calling out to him to let them have another chance.

Mom opened the door for me. I left the bike on the stoop, went in and started upstairs. Silently, Mom held the door for Ben. She closed it behind him. "Damn you, Ben," she said, "Damn you."

The next morning I took the bike outside and down to the other end of the projects where it would be harder for Mom to see me from the window, or even the stoop. The day before had been humiliating, but it had shown me something after all. I'd watched boys of all different sizes and shapes ride my bike, some of whom I knew were as old as I was and couldn't read or count. I understood the secret had to be in practice, not in intelligence. Now, I was determined.

When I got tired of falling, I decided to hide out behind the bushes awhile to rest. Even though there weren't any leaves on them, they were too dense for anyone to see me. When I pushed the bike through to the other side, Ray Anthony Robinson was standing behind the bushes, peeing and smoking a cigarette.

Ray Anthony lived across the courtyard with his mother in the 4B apartment building next to where we'd lived in 4A before we moved to the bungalows. Nobody was really sure how old Ray Anthony was, but Miss Helen, Mom's hairdresser, said she thought he had to be seventeen at least. He didn't go to high school and by law, you had to go until you were sixteen. Miss Helen said nobody she knew could remember a time when Ray Anthony had ever gone to school, but she was sure he must have. She whispered to my mother that Ray Anthony was "an out-and-out hood-lum." Miss Helen was always calling somebody's child a hoodlum, but I could tell from the way she said it that to be an "out-and-out hoodlum" was more serious than an ordinary run-of-the-mill hoodlum. So I stared at Ray Anthony after that from my window wondering what kind of crimes he might be on his way to commit.

When I pushed through the bushes to Ray Anthony Robinson standing there peeing and smoking, it felt like I'd pushed through to the other side of the world. He turned in my direction and aimed right through the spokes of my front tire. My eyes followed the arc back to where it came from, Ray Anthony Robinson's dick. It was long, wide and the color of these cookies Miss Odessa used to give me for dessert when I spent the night. Almond Macaroons. Most likely, Ray Anthony was the color of Almond Macaroons all over, but I'd never thought about it until I saw his dick. The way he looked at me, with his cigarette hanging from his lips and his waist pushed forward at me, you'd have thought it was the most natural thing in the world for us to be there, him peeing and me watching.

When he stopped peeing, he didn't put his dick back in his pants. He spat the cigarette in my direction, but he wasn't trying to hit me with it. He started peeing again, aiming at his cigarette until the smoke stopped spiraling up from it. I tried not to look impressed.

"Who gave you the girl's bike for Christmas?"

"It's not a girl's." It was hard to sound as forceful as I wanted, watching him slowly tuck himself back into his pants.

"You gonna let me ride it?"

He'd zipped his pants and I could look him in the face. I'd never been this close to Ray Anthony before, and he'd certainly never said anything to me. It was the first time I realized one of his two front teeth was chipped, just a little on the inside corner. He also had a big dent in his chin.

"No," I said. If I'd thought about it, I might have been scared to say no to him. But it seemed like he didn't expect me to say yes, he'd already figured out I'd say no, that wasn't the point of him asking. He walked closer to me and reached for the handlebars. That's when I saw his hair had a rusty, orange glow to it. I didn't like orange or red much. But Ray Anthony Robinson's hair was unlike any other reds or oranges I'd seen before.

"Leggo," he told me.

I smelled the cigarette on his breath, kept staring at the chipped tooth. I was filling in the space to see what he'd look like if he got it fixed.

"I can't let you ride it. My mom will see."

"I'll go the other way. Leggo."

I'd already let go. Ray Anthony pushed my bike through the bushes. I stood in the opening and watched him throw his leg over it easily without having to get a running start. He was wearing shoes with pointy toes and buckles on the sides. Pushing off, he huddled over the bars like the kids did when they raced each other. Except Ray Anthony wasn't racing anybody. He was just riding my bike wherever he'd decided to take it. I watched his butt lifted in the air and the muscles in his legs as he pumped the pedals. All I could do was wait behind the bushes and hope he wouldn't ride it in front of my house where Mom could see him, and that he'd bring it back. Soon.

I started to feel the cold for the first time that morning. But I couldn't move, playing the whole thing with Ray Anthony backwards and forwards in my mind. His cigarette was lying a few feet away. That and his footprints in the snow with the long, pointy toes were my evidence that he'd really been there.

But evidence wouldn't matter anyway. He hadn't beat

me up, knocked me down and ridden over me on my own bike. I was sure he'd seen me coming, sure that he'd waited till I could watch him, smoking and making bridges of piss in the air. But hoodlum or not, he'd told me only once, without sounding any more dangerous than my own mother, to let go of those handlebars. And I had. Without a fight, without even thinking about fighting him.

It might have been a half hour, it might have been longer before Ray Anthony brought my bike back, but by now, the time didn't matter. Whatever happened had happened already, before he left. It's the difference between when something begins and something continues. You can't compare the two.

When he pushed the bike back through the bushes, there was sweat running down from his thick bush of rust-colored hair and he had a perfectly folded handkerchief he kept patting his forehead with.

"You want me to ride you now? C'mon. Get behind me."

He was crazy. If I could get the bike away from him, the only thing I wanted to do was run home with it and tell my mother any lie I could think of to keep from coming outside again. The bike had attracted people I never would have spoken to or had anything to do with. If I couldn't lose it or give it away, I had to think of some excuse not to bring it out again anytime soon.

By the time I got home, Miss Odessa had already called Mom and told her she'd seen me behind the bushes with Ray Anthony Robinson. Told her she saw Ray Anthony ride away from the bushes on a red bicycle which by now the whole projects knew was mine. Mom asked me, "Well, what's your story, Louis?" but she was already in a mood to beat some behind.

"You gonna let everybody in the projects ride it but

you? I didn't spend months cleaning behind white men for that."

"He made me." I was looking at her, but I was picturing Ray Anthony Robinson with his chipped tooth, his rusty hair.

Mom started with her fists. "No, today was your fault. You can't blame today on anybody else." Then she grabbed the broom. She turned it upside down and used the stick part on me as my sister watched, looking troubled, but helpless.

The following Saturday morning Mom excused me from cleaning the apartment. "Take the bike outside and see how long you can hold on to it."

I wasn't out there five minutes before three kids started running toward me from the south end. I looked back at the window of our apartment. The curtains were pulled almost together. Mom was there, in the almost space.

The three kids formed a V at the front of the bike. Bubba Graves was on one side, this guy called Rat on the other, and some boy I'd never seen before who smelled bad, in the front. We all just looked at each other, like we were waiting for some kind of signal. The one who smelled bad walked in closer, straddling the front tire. He grabbed the handlebars and jerked the front of the bike so hard I was thrown to the side, but I held on and kept my balance so I didn't fall. The other two inched in closer to me.

"Better get the hell outta here." It was what I'd rehearsed to say to anybody about anything, the next time I got picked on.

"Who you cursin', faggot? You cursin' me?" The Smell leaned in over the handlebars so that we were eye to eye. I held my breath.

Rat said, "Yeah, he cursed you. I heard him curse you."

The Smell heaved the front of the bike toward Rat while Bubba Graves pushed it from the other side. Rat jumped out of the way as the bike fell over onto the snow with me halfway underneath it. I was still holding on to the handlebars. The three of them kicked the bike as I scrambled to get from under it. One, I couldn't see who, straddled me from behind with his legs around my neck and started kicking into my ribs with his heels. My ears started to ring. I squeezed my eyes shut, but the ringing only got louder.

"Get the hell off him! You hear me, you little bastard! Get off him now!" My mother's voice cut through.

Instead, he kicked me harder and faster. Each time Mom screamed, it got worse. If she doesn't stop, I thought, he'll kick a hole in my side.

But he stopped suddenly, and someone grabbed me under my arms and pulled me up from behind. I whirled around to try to free myself. It wasn't Bubba or Rat or The Smell who'd lifted me. It was Ray Anthony Robinson. He was in his undershirt. The first thing I saw was how much hair he had under his arm and how it was reddish colored too. Then, I saw my mother standing behind him.

I was dizzy, spitting snow, my head dropped toward the ground again. There was a bloody silhouette in the snow in the shape of a small rabbit.

"Why you gotta jump in for him?" The Smell shouted at Ray Anthony. "The faggot cursed me. Don't nobody curse me. I'm gonna kick his butt good."

"If you gonna kick somebody's butt, kick mine." I looked up to see Ray Anthony step toward him slowly with his legs spread wide, his thick arms swinging free. He was taller than any of us. He looked different to me now, like he was prepared to do whatever he had to to win. It wasn't the same as when he'd been behind the bushes. I realized for the first time that he probably hadn't even thought about hurting me that day. He'd just taken what he wanted, because he knew he could. I was ashamed to think he'd probably seen me get pushed around before. Why was he helping me now?

"Why you wanna front for a faggot, man? Let him fight for himself."

My body tensed with a new fear. Would The Smell convince Ray Anthony to leave me alone with them again? Please God, don't let Ray Anthony back down. I knew Mom would probably try to help me, but that would make it worse. They wouldn't fight her, but I'd get beat up again later on because she'd already called them some pretty rough names.

"Come on, you so bad." Ray Anthony stepped in closer to the kid. "Come on and kick my butt."

The Smell did step in closer to Ray Anthony, but my bike was between them. The Smell jumped on the bike so hard, he dented the back fender.

"You good-for-nothing little pig!" my mother shouted and grabbed a fallen tree branch near where she was standing. But The Smell was running backwards yelling, "You wait, faggot. You wait till your big red nigger ain't around."

Bubba and Rat backed off slowly, not even in the same direction as The Smell. The fear hadn't left me, though. I knew as far as Mom was concerned, there was still Ray Anthony to deal with. Saving me from getting my ribs kicked in didn't erase the fact that he'd taken a turn on my bike himself, the bike she said she'd cleaned behind white men to buy me.

"Well, looks like everybody in the projects is gonna ride that damn thing, or kill you trying."

She was talking to me, but glaring at Ray Anthony. He walked past her slowly, back toward his building. I stared at his arms hanging at his sides, wondering if he was cold with only his undershirt on. Maybe arms that looked like Ray Anthony's didn't get cold.

Mom was asking me, "You gonna pick up the bike or just leave it there so they can come back and get it?"

I stooped to pick it up, but I kept my eyes on Ray Anthony to see if he'd turn around before he went inside.

A few days after the bicycle fight, Mom looked out the window and saw Ray Anthony going across the courtyard. His mother was calling out the window to him, "Yeah, you go ahead and keep going! I don't want you back in here no way!"

Mom snapped the shade up higher and said to me without turning from the window, "You see him, don't you? You see him? That woman ought to call the army and tell them to come get his behind. That's just what she ought to do. I betcha Vietnam would straighten his hoodlum self out real good!"

Before, she'd only talked about what the army would do to *me*. I'd watch the seven o'clock news, seeing myself in the middle of all the shooting and fire. I'd never thought about anybody I knew being there, too.

I kept watching to see if Ray Anthony would come home that night, but I wasn't sure he had until the next day when I saw him coming out of 4B again. I put on my jacket and ran out, heading in the same direction he was, a little behind him, not saying anything though, not looking at him. When he got to the parking lot, he started walking faster. I couldn't keep up without him knowing I was following him.

"Ray Anthony!" I yelled. He didn't stop, but he slowed down and turned back to me. He was poking out his lips with a toothpick between them.

I had to know before I lost him, before he disappeared into the parking lot, with his hunched, muscly shoulders and his high-water pants. I needed to know if he'd be coming back.

"Are you going to Vietnam?"

This time he stopped. He looked at me like he didn't recognize who it was asking the question. It was too late to take it back.

"What you think?" He took the toothpick from between his lips and flicked it into the air as he turned away. "Am I goin' to somebody's Vietnam!"

As soon as I'd asked him, I knew how stupid it sounded. I'd seen those guys on the special live reports. In the helmets with the grass covering them, mud all over their faces. Ray Anthony would never look like that. It was hard enough to picture myself in those holes in the ground or running through fields beating the grass with a gun.

Besides, they didn't show that many black men in Vietnam on the news. Maybe the army wouldn't take me or Ray Anthony. Even if Ray Anthony's mother called the army like Mom said, if she could do such a thing, the army wasn't going to take Ray Anthony Robinson. And he knew it. That's why he looked at me like that. Because he knew. Right?

7

By eighth grade, Mom had come up with a plan that she said would keep me from getting murdered when I left our apartment. One night at dinner she announced, "Louis, Ben is going to teach you how to box." I looked up in protest, but she said, "It's already decided. We're going to start with an hour every Sunday after church."

I looked to the head of the table, hoping Ben would say he didn't want any part of this, but he was staring down at his plate as usual like a paying customer who'd stopped in to eat alone at a roadside diner.

"Every Sunday after church," Lorelle mimicked gaily. At four and a half, she amused herself by repeating pieces of conversations. Sometimes it was funny, sometimes I left the room so I wouldn't have to hear whatever she was repeating a second time.

"Ben's going to figure out how many rounds we'll have and how long each round will be."

"How long, how long each round will be," Lorelle sang. I excused myself from the table.

"Where're you going, Louis? There are still dishes to be washed."

"To the bathroom, ma'am. I'll do the dishes as soon as I get back."

Upstairs, I closed the door and sat on the side of the tub, sweating. It was only Wednesday, and the two of them had already figured out a way to ruin Sunday.

•   •   •

When we got home from church, before we were even inside the apartment, Mom said, "Don't take all day changing your clothes. Come down just as fast as you do to read those silly comic strips."

"What should I put on?" What was more to the point was, what do you want me to wear to let Ben knock the crap out of me in?

"Play clothes, of course. It's boxing, Louis. Use your head."

When I came back down, Mom had pushed the couch against one wall and the coffee table against the other. Lorelle was running around in circles, like she knew the living room was now Madison Square Garden.

Mom went to the foot of the stairs and yelled, "Ben? Are you ready? We're ready down here."

I'd seen their closed bedroom door when I was up there. I was hoping he'd sneaked out while we were at church. Maybe he wouldn't be back until it was so late they'd have to drag me out of bed for him to knock me around. At least then I'd have the excuse, I couldn't go to school exhausted from having to get up at midnight to box my stepfather.

When she saw that I'd put on jeans and an undershirt, Mom said, "You should have put on shorts like real boxers wear. Take off your T-shirt, at least. You've never seen a boxer in his undershirt, have you?"

Of course, Ben came downstairs in his undershirt and the pants he wore to fix things around the house. Why was it only me who had to be half naked for this circus?

Mom shrugged. "Suit yourself, then." She went into the kitchen and came back with a pitcher of water, two glasses and a couple of towels over her shoulder.

"Now Lorelle, you stay over here in this corner with Louis." Lorelle looked like she was being punished and didn't understand why. "Give him a glass of water when he's thirsty." Mom had planned out every detail. Ben probably didn't want to have anything more to do with Sunday boxing than I did.

"Louis, maybe you should do a few push-ups before you start. Get your energy up."

Maybe *you* should do a few push-ups, Mom. Why are you doing this?

Ben got down on his knees so that now he was only about a head taller than me. That was supposed to make us even, make the whole thing fair. He still may as well have been Rat or Bubba Graves or any of the baboons who knocked me around out in the courtyard. The only advantage, if you could call it that, was that Ben would get to punch me without anybody but Mom and Lorelle watching. Mom told me she'd seen me get beat up from every window in the apartment, front and back. The difference was, she'd never set it up before so she'd be guaranteed a good seat when it happened.

"Each round is going to be three minutes. Okay?"

"Yes, ma'am." My legs felt like they were melting down into my sneakers. Ben took off his watch. Jesus, he's going to kill me, I thought. He's going to kill me and he doesn't want to hurt his precious watch.

"Put your dukes up, Louis." Mom lit a cigarette and left it hanging from one side of her mouth. She raised a glass above her head and clinked a spoon against it hard and fast and for so long, I was sure it would shatter and rain down onto her face. "Round one!" she shouted.

At first, I just stood there in front of him. I knew enough to hold my fists in front of my face in case he threw a punch, but I wasn't going to try to hit him. Mom called to me, "Get a punch in, Louis. At least *try* to get a punch in."

I started bobbing around like fighters I'd seen on television, thinking maybe I could stall until the three minutes were up.

Even on his knees, Ben blocked me no matter what direction I went toward him from. I couldn't have hit him even if I'd wanted to, but I thought the dance I was doing made me *look* like I wasn't afraid of him. When she clanked for round two, Mom said, "Louis, don't let Lorelle see you being such a coward. Don't make her ashamed of her big brother."

Lorelle was holding the glass Mom had given her toward me with her chubby hands wrapped around it. "Here, Louis. Drink your water. Don't fight Daddy. You're gonna make him beat you up."

By the time Mom called round three, Ben must've decided he was bored kneeling there in front of me. He hadn't had much to do except keep his fists up in the air in case I ever got the guts to hit him. Now, he decided he wasn't waiting anymore. He reached out and slapped me so hard the whole side of my head from temple to jaw felt like he'd knocked it off my face. My mouth went bone dry. The room seemed to tilt so it felt like I was climbing the floor. Either I'd been knocked deaf or there wasn't a sound in the room for what felt like a very long time.

Finally Mom said, "God, Ben, Wha'd you do that for? Look at his face. Look what you did to his face."

Ben reached for me. I ducked away from him, but Mom grabbed my jaw from the other side.

"He's bleeding, Ben. For god's sake, what did you do to him?!"

She swung my head around and Ben took hold of my

face, his hand a leathery catcher's mitt, pulling me toward him.

"It's just a scratch. Probably from my ring." He let go of me and stared down at his high school ring. Why had the big gorilla taken off his watch and not his ring?

Mom ran upstairs and brought down the bottle of witch hazel. She poured some onto a washcloth. "Here. Hold this on your face." She went to the kitchen to get ice.

"You must've hit him pretty damn hard, Ben. It's starting to swell."

"It wasn't hard at all. If I'd hit him hard, he'd be unconscious." Ben rolled his eyes at me. He stood up, brushed off his knees and went toward the stairs. Mom ran after him. I was sure she'd continue to yell at him for hitting me so hard in the face. I wanted to hear her say she must've been crazy to let it happen in the first place.

"Ben," she called hoarsely. "Ben, where are you going? I'm going to put dinner on the table now. Right now. Do you hear me?"

Ben didn't answer. Mom went into the kitchen and started serving plates loudly until we were all sitting around the table staring down at them in front of us mumbling, "Let us thank Him for this food." The only plate she left empty was her own. She stood at the stove smoking cigarettes one after the other. I could smell from where I was sitting at the table, there was whiskey in her teacup.

When I looked up at her to ask if I could be excused from the table, her eyes were red with black makeup smudges around them, her face shiny with sweat. There were tiny bits of white tissue across her forehead and under her bottom lip, a trail from the crumbling paper napkin she kept wiping herself with. She sat with me in the kitchen as I washed and dried the dishes, but we didn't say anything to each other. For several nights afterward, I fell asleep picturing her like that, trying to guess what she'd been thinking.

Friday, when I came home from school she told me, "Ben and I have decided the Sunday boxing matches are a good idea. You know he's sorry about scratching you with his ring, don't you? God knows I've seen you lay down for worse out there. This Sunday, try to make me proud of you. You give him a few good licks this time. Alright?"

Sunday after Sunday, I tried. Sometimes for Mom. Sometimes for Lorelle. Sometimes for anybody I could make up in my mind, smiling over in the corner, cheering me on. Just so I could get to the end of the round.

8

It wasn't what you'd call an invitation. Ernestine Buggman told Mom about her daughter Delilah having a party for her sixteenth birthday and Mom assured Mrs. Buggman, "Louis will be there. Just tell me what time."

She wasn't concerned that Delilah Buggman hardly knew I was alive—actually, Delilah did know I was alive—she and two of her girlfriends had watched the bicycle episode with Bubba and the others trying to bury me under the snow. The important thing to Mom, though, was that this party was another step toward Manhood. And if not Manhood, "At least," she told me, "it's a chance for you to get a couple of those damn criminals out there on your side."

Mom made me take a bath for the party and laid out on my bed what she wanted me to wear. White shirt, navy blue dress pants, and a red sweater vest with two reindeer on the front that I'd rolled up and hidden in the back of my drawer. None of this would have been my choice if I'd had one. I wasn't invited to parties, but I'd watched enough guys from my window on Friday and Saturday nights to know that no one would be wearing anything close to to what Mom had decided on for me.

She bought a pink blouse from Saks for me to give to Delilah. I knew Delilah wouldn't like it, because it was neither orange nor purple, the only two colors I'd ever seen her wear.

Mrs. Buggman told Mom the party was at eight. I was sure no one would get there on time, so when Mom shoved me out the door at 7:45, I walked around for an hour until I got too cold to do anything but go ahead to Delilah's. Luckily, I got there at the same time as three older kids I didn't know. Delilah opened the door and said hi to the girl in front of me and the two boys behind as though there was no one in between. Well, not exactly. She did snatch the present Mom had wrapped in pink foil paper from me. I wanted to tell her I knew she'd hate it, but I didn't say anything to her either. I especially didn't thank her for inviting me to her party like Mom said to make sure I remembered to. I went over to a corner where I could watch the clock on the wall. Mom told me I had to stay an hour. I wanted to make sure I knew when my hour was up.

The only other person in the room was a guy in the corner playing records. Delilah and the kids who'd come the same time I had started dancing immediately. What was Delilah doing before we got there, I wondered, with her own personal disc jockey playing records in an empty living room? I made a job for myself handing the guy whatever record he called for next. When that wasn't enough to keep me busy, I pulled my sweater out of my coat sleeve where I'd stuffed it and used it to dust off the records that looked like they needed it.

About a dozen records later, the room was filled with a few older kids from outside the projects. To my relief, I didn't know most of them at all. The guys who knew me looked like they couldn't believe Delilah had invited me. I kept dusting records with this expression that was supposed to say, "I'm getting paid to be here. I'm with the dj. Otherwise, I wouldn't be caught dead at this stinkin' party."

I heard Delilah say her mother had gone out and I thought about how Mom was so sure Mrs. Buggman would be there. The room was hot, the air heavy with the smells of hair oil and deodorant. Beer was being passed around in paper cups, but nobody'd given me any. Delilah brought the disc jockey two tumblers full and told him, "Time to play something slow, Cee-Cee."

She turned all the lamps off, except for one with a blue bulb. Cee-Cee put on this song called "In a Trance" and the kids started to slow-dance. If you could call it that. Nothing much was moving on anybody except their butts. Pushing into each other, barely moving, hip to hip making figure eights. Push, push. Push, push. The guys had their fingers clamped over the tops of the girls' behinds. Push, push. Push, push. And everybody was sweating. A lot. Delilah was dancing with some guy who looked older than anyone else in the room. He had on a tight shirt, shiny pants and a little hat that were all the same color green. He wore the hat with the brim pulled down over one eye. Delilah had both of her eyes closed. Push. Push. Shiny Pants put his hand up under her sweater and I looked away.

When "In a Trance" was over, Shiny Pants called to Cee-Cee, "You know what to do!" and Cee-Cee played it again. He didn't seem to mind. He laughed and said something under his breath about Shiny Pants trying to cop an extra feel, but I started humming so he wouldn't think I heard him. That's when I looked up at the door and saw Ray Anthony Robinson.

He didn't come all the way into the apartment. He eased in against the wall so that he was right next to the doorway, leaning with his thumbs in his pockets and his hips thrust out into the room the same way he had when

I'd first seen him, behind the bushes. He had a little hat on too, like the guy dancing with Delilah, except his was black. It occurred to me those hats and the way they wore them made Ray Anthony and the guy push pushing with Delilah look like the only two men in a room full of boys.

Ray Anthony's pants were shiny, too. Gray, shiny and hugging his butt.

"Will ya gimme, gimme one more chance? / your ooo ooo love has me in a trance."

Ray Anthony saw me, he had to see me sitting across the room from him. In the dark. In the corner. Next to the record player. I kept dusting the 45 in my lap round and round with my reindeer sweater, trying not to stare at him. When I knew Cee-Cee wasn't looking, I took a few swallows from one of the cups he hadn't touched yet.

"In a Trance" was over. Cee-Cee put on a fast one.

"Baby, baby, come on, come on / Baby, baby, 'cause your love's so strong."

I threw my head around to the drums and sang along. I knocked my knees together in time. What I really wanted to do was ask Ray Anthony Robinson if he'd dance with me. The floor was crowded now. I couldn't find him across the floor anymore. So I took another quick gulp of beer and stood. I got up for the first time since I'd come in and leaned against the wall like I'd seen Ray Anthony do. There he was. I looked right at him. I wanted to wave to him, but I didn't. I smiled, though. I tapped my foot, bobbed my neck, twisted my hips. And I smiled at Ray Anthony Robinson. Singing in my high voice, "Baby, baby come on, come on."

After a while, Delilah came over to the record player, whispered to Cee-Cee and he nodded. He pulled a small flashlight out of his jacket pocket. Delilah went and turned the blue light off so that now the room was completely dark. Somebody snickered. One girl squealed, "Oh no you *won't!*" and I saw her silhouette when she opened the door to the apartment and hurried out.

I looked toward the wall where Ray Anthony had been standing, but I couldn't see him anymore. Cee-Cee nudged me.

"You hold the flashlight."

My hand was kind of shaky, but I was glad I still had a job. Now Cee-Cee was only playing slow songs.

"If you, if you need me to / I'll sure nuff play the fool for you" and "Lay down baby, by my side / Love's gonna keep you satisfied."

After the third record was over I held my breath, knowing that was when I was supposed to point the flashlight down to the floor between my legs so it wouldn't glare out into the room. Instead, I held it up and pointed it at the wall next to the door. Yes! Ray Anthony was still there. Alone. The light hit his face. He covered his eyes.

"What the—?!" he yelled. I dropped the flashlight. It rolled toward Delilah's couch, but I dove to the floor as fast as I could and caught it.

"I'm sorry. I'm really sorry," I said, holding the light to my chest. But nobody else said anything. When Cee-Cee started the next record, the apartment door opened. In the hall light I could see Ray Anthony from behind. Then he was gone.

I couldn't run out after him like I wanted to. Even if I had the guts, I'd just done something so stupid, what could I have said to make up for it? Suddenly, it all struck me as too horrible to be anything but funny. I wouldn't worry about it at all until I got home and got some sleep. I reached down and grabbed Cee-Cee's beer. Finishing it,

I tried to imagine what it would've been like to dance with Ray Anthony in the glow of the blue light. Softly, I sang into the plastic tumbler, "Baby, baby, come on, come on / Baby, baby, 'cause your love's so strong."

9

"I've got to get Lorelle out of this place," I heard Mom tell Ben one night. "They've damn near killed Louis. I'll go to jail before I let one of them put their hands on my little girl."

This was the beginning of Mom's campaign to get out of the projects, one way or another. "Moving," "someplace better" and "getting out" became a part of every conversation she had with us. At dinner, she started as soon as Ben sat down to eat. When he jumped up before anyone else was finished to get away from the table, she told him, "I know you don't want to hear me talk about getting out of here again. But it doesn't matter. We are going to, whether you help me or not."

I waited until he'd left for work one day and asked her why Ben didn't want to get out of the projects himself.

"All Ben can do is count pennies and come up short. That's who Ben is. But it will take more than not having money to keep me here."

Their fights about it got louder and more frequent. She'd accuse him of lying about how much money he had and he'd laugh at her. "Yeah, I'm a liar. A millionaire liar. I got millions, more than millions."

I'd wake up in the middle of the night to her screaming at him about it. Once, it got so bad I ran into their bedroom and yelled, "All she wants to do is move out of this shit hole! Why can't you help her?"

Mom called out to me, "Go back to your room, Louis. Go back, now!" Ben leapt out of bed and backed me into a corner. He sneered. "She asked me to help her by marrying her. She thought it would help *you* too. But the two of you do whatever you please, don't you? Nobody can help either one of you because you both know everything. And what does it get you? If the two of you are too good to live here, let's see what you can do about it."

The next day I apologized to Mom. She told me, "Don't ruin it, Louis. Don't ruin what I'm trying to do."

Suddenly, she started to change how she talked to Ben about moving, although it was still all I ever heard her talk to him about. She laughed now, as if moving was definite, it was only a matter of time. She flirted with him about how different everything would be when it happened. I almost believed he'd agreed to it, except as soon as he wasn't around, she was nervous and mean as if all the laughing and flirting was harder work than she'd ever had to do and she wasn't sure how much longer she could keep it up.

She didn't speak to me much during this time at all except to let me know there was nothing I did that couldn't have been done faster or better. Saturday morning, after we'd cleaned most of the apartment, she called me into the kitchen for lunch and handed me a ham sandwich.

"This Friday after school, I'm gonna let you do something special." I was surprised at how gentle she sounded, but suspicious because for weeks I hadn't been able to do anything even close to right.

"You're going to spend the weekend with your grandfather. I'll put you on the train Friday afternoon and you'll come back Sunday." She was leaning away from me at the table, watching me. "What do you think about that?"

I didn't know what to say. "Yes, ma'am" was all I could come up with.

"What's that supposed to mean?" Mom pushed farther back in her chair. I knew she was ready to explode no matter what I said. I got up from the table quickly so that our eyes couldn't meet.

"Nothing, ma'am." I turned the water on full force, began to wash my plate. She stood and stepped closer toward me at the sink. I kept my eyes lowered, concentrating on sponging the plate, hoping she'd turn away. Finally, she sighed loudly and walked out.

When I finished, I could feel her waiting for me in the next room. I still hadn't figured out what else I could say about going to New York, to my grandfather's. I didn't feel like I knew him. He was about seventy, I guessed. Mom would call him on his birthday and Ben drove us into the city a few days before or after Thanksgiving and Christmas to see him. The most I ever said to him was "Hi, Grandaddy, how are you? School is fine," and then I sat by his window and stared out at 162nd Street until it was time to go back to Stratfield. Mom and Ben didn't say much more than I did. Sometimes the visits were so short, the drive to New York didn't make sense. I asked Mom once why she bothered if she wasn't going to stay longer. She'd rolled her eyes at me. "I certainly hope you figure out the answer by the time I get to be as old as he is." She invited him to come to Stratfield to spend the holidays with us, but he never did.

When I asked her about my grandmother, she said, "They weren't together. It was my father who raised me. I didn't know my mother until I was as old as you are now." She looked up toward the ceiling and smoothed the front of her neck. Her hand slid slowly down her chest and into her lap.

"Did she. . . is she alive now?" I asked.

"No . . . there was an accident, a car accident."

"Was she alone?"

Mom didn't answer. It was risky, I knew, to continue to question her. I wasn't sure we'd ever talk about it again though, so I took the risk.

"Before the accident," I asked, "do you remember . . . anything about her?"

"What I remember most is the first time I saw her. Us looking at each other like strangers and me not wanting to feel that way when that's exactly what we were."

Mom lit a cigarette, even though there was already one burning, dropping ashes from the ledge over the sink.

"I remember everything we said to each other from that first day to the last. I remember everything." But what she remembered was private. I understood. I wouldn't ask her about my grandmother again.

I decided I would tell Mom that I wanted to go to see my grandfather so she wouldn't have something else to hold against me, but I didn't get the chance. When I went into the living room, she was on her knees polishing the couch legs. Without looking up she said, "I figured your being around another man couldn't hurt. Better than you hiding in your room from Friday to Sunday."

During the week, I grew more excited about going away. I'd never taken the train alone. Once I got to my grandfather's, I probably wouldn't do anything but home-work. The rest of the time I'd listen to the radio or sit looking out the window. He didn't have a television. Still, it would be someplace different and it was only for the weekend. If I was lucky, I'd get home too late Sunday for boxing with Ben. That alone would make it worth it.

Friday, Mom insisted on making a tag to pin on me with my name, address and a note that said in case of emergency she should be contacted. Even she thought it was pretty funny after she'd pinned it on my jacket, but she still insisted I wear it.

"You may think thirteen is a grown man, Louis, but the law doesn't. If anything should happen to you, nobody would think, 'Oh well, he was a grown man. Nobody was responsible for him being on that train but him.' I'm your mother. I'm the one they'd come for."

I didn't know what she imagined might happen, but as I packed, I pictured the train I'd be on in a slow-motion collision. We were on a high bridge above a river. Passengers tumbled through the windows toward the water like rag dolls. The last one to fall was me, the tag Mom made around my neck a weight, strangling me, pulling me deeper into the water.

"Remember to look for your grandfather as soon as you get off. If you don't see him, stand there and wait until you do." With her hand on my behind, Mom pushed me up the stairs of the train. I turned and waved down to her on the platform, excited to be leaving her there. "It should take a little over an hour," she called up to me. Don't fall asleep or you'll go all the way downtown to Grand Central Station."

She'd made sure I was on an express so the next stop after ours would be 125th Street. Expresses skipped all the little towns in between Stratfield and New York. That way, she said, there'd be fewer strangers on the train with me going into the city.

It was pretty crowded, anyway. I found an empty two-seater, though, and put my bag down beside me hoping I could ride all the way to New York without anyone in the other seat. I watched Mom on the other side of the rain-streaked window, chasing the train as it pulled away, calling out all the things she'd already told me a hundred times. "Wait in one place for your grandfather to find you. Don't take off your tag. Don't talk to anyone on the train except the conductor. If your grandfather never shows up, find a policeman."

As soon as the train glided past her and Stratfield began to disappear, I reached up to undo the safety pin that fastened the tag to my jacket.

"You wouldn't mind some company, would you?"

The first thing I thought was how small he was, not as small as me, but no bigger, no taller than David Pecchio, the tallest boy in my class. His cheeks were flushed, plum colored, veiled by a patchy, ragged shadow of a beard. His hair was wet looking and smashed down on his head the way the white boys in school wore theirs, with some of it sticking up in the back like overgrown crabgrass too tough to be bullied by a lawnmower.

He reached for my suitcase. There was nothing I could think of to say to stop him. He was so short, he had to jump to put it on the rack above us. I imitated Ben's sneer. Wrinkled-up suit. Looked like gray pajamas. His briefcase was new looking though, like a big leather envelope. Oxblood. That was the color in Ben's shoebox that Mom told me to shine my loafers with until Ben said I should buy my own polish. Oxblood was what the guy in the wrinkled suit would use on his briefcase if he wanted it to look better than his suit did.

"Ed. Ed MacMillan." He held out his hand. It was

small and pale and I could tell he bit his nails. They weren't bloody or disgusting like some nail biters', but you could definitely tell he spent a lot of time with his fingers in his mouth. I wasn't real anxious to shake his hand, but I tried to make it strong and look directly into his eyes like Mom taught me.

"Louis Bowman." My voice was higher then I'd aimed for.

"Hi, Louis." He smiled. He had those teeth where the front four are flat and even and the next two on either side overlap. "I heard your mother back there on the platform at Stratfield. She's pretty worried about you getting to New York in one piece, isn't she?" He placed his briefcase flat across his lap.

I knew Mom had been loud enough for people to hear. Now it felt like she was following me. This was a test to see if I'd disobey her by talking to a stranger so soon after she'd told me not to.

"Makes you feel like a big baby, right? Like she doesn't trust you." He took off his glasses and rubbed the bridge of his nose. It was bad enough he'd moved my bag and sat down when I wanted to ride alone. Now this little white man in the rumpled suit was talking about my mother and me like he knew us.

"Nothing like your own mother to make you feel dumb. Like she's forgotten how old her own kid is." He reached inside his jacket and pulled out his glasses case. He slid his glasses in, then slowly ran two fingers back and forth over the case as if he was reading braille. He put it back inside his jacket.

"How old are you?"

He reeked of aftershave lotion. It smelled bitter like lemon mixed with perfume, different from Ben's blue,

Windex-looking cologne that smelled more like witch hazel. I guessed this guy put on so much extra because of the beard. I wondered if it would ever fill in or if he was satisfied with the way it was.

It might have been easier to talk to him if he hadn't already brought Mom into it. Now, I thought, no matter what I say he'll know I've disobeyed her. Still, I couldn't sit there and let him think I was too retarded to even say how old I was.

"Thirteen," I told him. Then I turned as much of my body as I could to the window to let him know there wouldn't be any more conversation.

"Eighth grade, right?"

I nodded, not even a whole nod. A half nod.

"I was the smallest kid in my class when I was in eighth grade, even smaller than most of the girls. A shrimp. And boy, did they give me a rough way to go. It felt like the whole school was a war zone. I was on one side and everybody else was on the other."

His voice seemed almost as high as my own, except he whined. He'd probably sounded the same way when he was in eighth grade.

"Talk about feeling dumb. You know I just got off the train from New York in Stratfield and now I have to go right back?" Without waiting for my answer, he continued. "I was supposed to study a report over the weekend for a meeting on Monday. So what do you think I leave smack in the middle of my desk? The damn report, of course. Can you believe that?" I liked that he said "damn." He wasn't treating me like a kid.

"I tell ya, this has been some helluva week. My nerves are shot. Look how my hand is shaking. Look!"

I turned to look at his chewed-on hand, which might

have been trembling on its own, but he was obviously exaggerating it. When I didn't laugh, he let the shaking take over his whole body, his legs outstretched in front of him like a ventriloquist's dummy. I smiled and shook my head.

His head fell back as he grinned. Just as quickly, he dropped his hand onto my leg. I jumped in surprise, then looked straight ahead, feeling his fingers squeezing just above my knee. They squeezed tighter, but I didn't move or say anything.

"This is an express train to New York next stop one hundred and twenty-fifth street may I have all tickets please."

Ed MacMillan looked over his shoulder, I guess to see how close the conductor was. I expected him to take his hand away, but he didn't. It was as if he was playing a game of Dare with himself. I wasn't playing, but I was in it, sitting there next to him with my leg frozen under his hand.

"All tickets please." The conductor was right behind us. Ed MacMillan lifted his hand very slowly off my leg. He undid the fastening on his briefcase and felt around in it without looking inside. Pulled out a small card that had about ten holes punched in it. When he did, I saw his wedding ring, a tiny gold thread that looked like it still might be a little big for his finger.

The conductor reached past him and took my ticket. "Next stop is one twenty-fifth."

"Yes. Thank you," I said.

Ed MacMillan elbowed me and smiled. He held the card up. The conductor took it and punched another hole in it. He stepped ahead to the next seat. I waited, as though Ed MacMillan had started to say something to me, but hadn't finished. I counted as the conductor moved one, two, three seats away from us. When he got to the fourth seat ahead of us, Ed MacMillan, without a word or even looking in my direction, put his hand back on my leg, only higher this time, and moved his fingers slowly but firmly, massaging my thigh.

I was embarrassed and ashamed to realize my dick was getting hard. The first thing I thought was that I didn't want Ed MacMillan to know.

Most of the time, I tried not to think about my dick at all. The guys in the projects talked about their dicks all the time. Even Mom talked about dicks more than I did, except she called them "googies."

In second grade, two boys' mothers had been called in by the principal because the boys had been caught in the coatroom before school showing each other their dicks. I'd thought it was a pretty dumb game to begin with and couldn't understand why it was being given so much attention, but when I told Mom about it, she was even more upset by what had happened than Miss Sanderhuff, the teacher, had been. She stopped ironing in the middle of the story and when I finished, she came over to where I was standing. She grabbed me by the shoulder so hard I winced, thinking I was going to get a beating for repeating it.

"If I ever hear about you and any googie business, you'll be sorry. You understand?"

What I understood was how embarrassing it was to have my mother talk to me about dicks and call them something that made the conversation even more ridiculous. When I'd wash my hands for dinner in the bathroom and come out to the table, she'd ask, "Did you shake your googie?" Or, once when I'd tried on a pair of shorts at Rudy's Sporting Goods, she'd giggled in front of the salesman and a couple of other customers, "Those are so short, your googie will be hanging out."

Our last big "googie" conversation came when I was twelve. I was sent home early one day from school, determined not to admit I had diarrhea from wolfing down six large chocolate bars for lunch instead of the tuna fish sandwich Mom had sent with me. I told her I'd been excused because I just wasn't feeling well.

"Headache?" she asked.

"No, ma'am."

"Stomachache?"

"Sort of."

She stared at me for a minute, her eyes like searchlights moving up and down my body. Finally, she asked, "It doesn't have anything to do with your googie, does it?"

I answered no as quickly and as definite sounding as I could so she wouldn't pursue it.

"Cause if it is, I can have Ben talk to you about it. Or we can make an appointment with the doctor."

"Please, Mom. It has nothing to do with that. Please."

She let it go, but I thought about it for a long time, trying to figure out how she'd come up with the question and why the heck she was still calling it a googie when I was twelve years old. Everybody I knew including girls and other people's mothers, especially in the projects, called it a dick. So what did Mom think she was doing?

Sitting there on the train with Ed MacMillan's hand squeezing my thigh, it was definitely my dick and not my googie that was hard. What made me more nervous than him knowing was the idea that back in Stratfield, Mom somehow knew that it was happening. She was sitting at home watching everything, like the witch with the crystal ball in *The Wizard of Oz*. She'd tell me she'd seen everything as soon as I got home on Sunday.

"I'm awfullly glad to meet you, Louis Bowman. Since

83

you're a commuter too, we'll have to figure out a way for you to come to Forty-Ninth Street to see my office sometime. It's on the twenty-third floor. I swear, you can see half the world from my window. We'll get you behind my desk so you can see what that feels like. Sound interesting to you?"

I didn't answer. It sounded ridiculous and exciting at the same time.

"Or maybe since we both live in Stratfield, we'll run into each other there."

What happened to the office visit so quickly? I'd never been to anyone's office in New York before. Half the world from his window? He was exaggerating, but I supposed there had to be some truth in it. Had he changed his mind because I hadn't said yes right away? Through all of it, he never took his hand off my thigh. Squeezing. Almost letting go. Squeezing harder. Tighter. Not quite letting go.

"I'm hoping I'll see you again. Are you hoping you'll see me again?"

When the conductor called 125th Street, Ed MacMillan stood up and pulled my suitcase down from the overhead rack. I looked past him out the window and saw, among a wide cluster of black and brown faces, my grandfather standing on the platform watching for me. It was as if I'd fallen asleep looking through this same window at my mother and woke up with my grandfather in the place where my mother had been. In between was a strange dream I wouldn't be able to tell anyone.

Ed MacMillan took my suitcase and started toward the door of the train with it. I jumped up and followed. As we stood waiting for the train to stop, there were other black people waiting to get off at 125th Street. A few of them stared at Ed MacMillan and me. I wanted him to give me my suitcase and go sit down so I could go back to being who I was. Louis Bowman going to spend the weekend with his grandfather. Not some kid who rode from Stratfield to New York with a white man squeezing his thigh.

When the train stopped, I grabbed my suitcase from him, but not before he put his hand on my shoulder and asked, "You alright?"

"Yes," I said. The conductor jumped onto the platform before the train came to a full stop. He reached up and took my bag from me. Grandaddy was a few feet behind him. He wasn't smiling or waving or doing anything that looked like he knew me. Quickly, I looked back over the heads of the other passengers getting off the train. Ed MacMillan was still standing there, grinning down at me. And again, because I couldn't smile back at him, I stared at his teeth instead.

10

From that Friday afternoon until Sunday when I took the 4:05 express back to Stratfield, Grandaddy and I sat in his apartment in almost total silence. I sat next to the window, looking from my book to the street, listening to the familiar sounds of kids calling to each other in nicknames and curse words.

Grandaddy stayed in his room most of the time. I peeked in when I went past it to the bathroom. He had taken apart a radio and spread its insides out all over the bed. There was another radio playing quietly on his dresser. All news. No music. He didn't look up when I went by.

Mom told me he'd only gone to the fifth grade down South. His father had died in his twenties while working on a white man's farm and Grandaddy had to drop out of school to help support his mother and younger sister.

"Your grandfather only talked about it once that I remember," Mom told me. "He said his father sat down to rest in the middle of the afternoon, leaned back against a wooden post he'd just put into the ground and died right there. Seems like his heart gave out. And he wasn't thirty years old." I was curious for more details of this story. I wanted to know, for instance, what kind of work Grandad had done when he was even younger than I was, but I wasn't sure I'd ever get comfortable enough with him to ask anything at all.

Friday night, we ate a chicken casserole Mom had sent

on the train with me. On Saturday, I volunteered to make spaghetti with a canned sauce, but Grandaddy said there was plenty of casserole left. We sat across from each other in his kitchen. It smelled like gas was leaking from the stove. I stared at a mousetrap in the corner, hoping no mice would come out while we were sitting there. Every few minutes I'd shift my feet under the table just to make some kind of noise.

After dinner I washed the dishes like I would have at home, and went into the other room to sit by the window. I sat by myself in the dark, watching Harlem like it was a movie. There had to have been more black people living on 162nd Street than in all of Stratfield. If you lived in Harlem your whole life and didn't watch any television like my grandfather, you could probably come to believe that most of the world was black. Maybe half the world was what somebody else saw from a window on 49th Street, but what about all the people in my Harlem movie? If you couldn't see them from your window, how could you be so sure you were looking at half the world?

Grandaddy started talking to me from his bedroom. He didn't call my name or come to the door. He said, "I know Jeanette sees you get to church on Sundays."

I figured I should get up and go to his room to answer him. He was sitting on the side of his bed, smoking a cigar.

"Yes, sir." Mom had said my missing church was the only thing she regretted about me being in New York on the weekend.

"There's a church around the corner on a Hundred Sixty-first," Grandaddy told me. "You're big enough to go on over there in the morning, if you want."

I wasn't sure if he was ordering me to go or giving me a choice.

"No thank you, sir," I said, trying to make it sound like I didn't want to inconvenience him by going.

"Suit yourself." He never looked up from the newspaper.

That night I dreamed about Ed MacMillan. He and I were sitting on the stoop outside Grandaddy's building. I wanted to show him how many more black people there were in Harlem than in Stratfield where we both lived. But he wouldn't pay attention to what I was saying. He kept making jokes about leaving reports on his desk and how absentminded he was. I thought what I was saying was important, but he wasn't listening. I was annoyed. How could you be so absentminded, I wanted to ask him, and have an office that overlooks half the world?

Sunday afternoon, when Grandaddy and I were standing on the platform above 125th Street waiting for the 4:05, I wondered if Ed MacMillan might be on the train going back. Maybe sometimes he had to work on Sundays. I reached down and put my hand on my leg, gripped my thigh as tight as I could, but I didn't have Ed MacMillan's strength.

"You listen to me." Grandaddy surprised me. He sounded like I'd suddenly done something wrong.

"You behave yourself. Don't give Jeanette any trouble. You do what her and Ben tell you to do." I was stunned. There was a tingling in my jaw. I held it tight to keep it from quivering.

"Jeanette said she got Ben to give you some boxing lessons and you're acting real sissyish about it. You don't know anything about how to take care of yourself, do you?"

"No, Grandad."

"You should be grateful you got somebody to take that kind of interest in you."

"Yes, Grandad." Grateful. For getting knocked around at the end of every week.

"You're sposed to be a man. Act like one."

We stood in silence until the 4:05 pulled in.

"I'll call Jeanette, tell her you're on the train like I said I would." I turned and waved, wondering what he'd tell her about the weekend. It hadn't been bad, sitting there, reading homework chapters and staring out the window. It absolutely beat being home with Ben and Mom. Still, I wanted to know many times they'd agreed on for these visits.

"You're sposed to be a man. Act like one." I watched Grandaddy leaving the platform before my train pulled off. I thought about the men I knew. The two I thought of immediately were Ben and Ray Anthony. Grandaddy probably wouldn't consider Ray Anthony a man, but I did. I smiled thinking what Grandad would say if I acted more like Ray Anthony Robinson. You told me to act like a man, Grandad, I thought. You didn't say which one.

11

Mom and Ben seemed to be getting along better than usual. Sunday night, she was too busy fussing over his dinner to ask me anything about New York. After we ate, she rubbed his back and shoulders, wanting to know if she'd cooked the roast too long. She was working harder than she did when she scrubbed floors on her knees.

I wondered if my being out of the apartment for the weekend had made that much of a difference for them. If the way she was practically ignoring me after I got home was any evidence, I'd be spending a lot more weekends on 162nd Street. For all the attention she was giving him, though, I still didn't believe Ben could be persuaded to do anything he didn't want to. Mom would be furious, I thought, if all these back rubs and special recipes didn't get her a house.

"I had a good time with Grandaddy," I lied to her.

"Yeah, well, I'll send you back if my money holds out." She didn't bring up Sunday boxing, and I didn't remind her.

The next weekend she did send me back, but this time Ed MacMillan wasn't on the train. Nothing felt like it had the week before. I sat on Grandaddy's couch for hours, bored by the sights and sounds of Harlem that had been so magical to me the week before.

It was worse the week after that. I decided Mom must really be kidding herself into thinking getting me out of the apartment would get her a house. On the train ride home, I wished I could tell her I didn't want to go back to my grandfather's again and she should find some other way of making me disappear.

By this time, she'd decided she trusted me enough to catch a city bus home from the train station. It was only about a twenty-minute wait, the bus let me off near the projects, and I walked the rest of the way home. The station was run-down and stale smelling. No one seemed to spend very much time inside, except to buy a ticket. I wouldn't have gone in to wait for the bus that third Sunday if it hadn't been raining.

There were two women waiting for the bus like I was. They were standing together on one side of the station, I was alone on the other. When I realized the bus was more than a few minutes late, I decided to call Mom from one of the pay phones. I held the greasy-looking receiver away from my ear and dialed. I could hear it ringing when I saw the door of the men's room open a few feet away from the phone booths. Hurrying my way, although he didn't seem to see me, was Ed MacMillan. I hung up the phone and stepped out of the booth into his path.

"Hi!"

Ed MacMillan stopped just short of knocking me over. He was wearing a plaid shirt and a navy blue windbreaker and jeans. He looked even younger without his wrinkled gray suit on. He seemed nervous now, too, so unlike the Ed MacMillan from that first Friday on the train.

"Hi." He remembered me, but he wasn't as glad to see me as I thought he'd be. "What are you doing here? You by yourself?" He looked around the empty station.

"Yep. I just came back from New York." I was ready to stand right there for as long as it took to get to know exactly who he was.

"Well, it's good to see you again."

He was already past me when I ran backward and blurted, "I go to my grandfather's every weekend. I always come home on the same train. The 4:05."

He didn't respond. But he looked at me, really looked at me and I knew he'd heard what I'd said. Then he hurried through the station without looking back.

Through the station window I watched him get into a dirty, cream-colored station wagon. There was a bright green bumper sticker on the front fender that said "The Whole Family Plays at Playland." He's got kids, I thought, as he drove away from the station. He's going home to his kids.

I changed my mind again about being sent to New York on weekends. It occurred to me that whether I was on my way or coming back, things were different than when I was in Stratfield. Even when I was being ignored at Grandad's, it was better than being at home knowing Mom wished I wasn't there. And boredom definitely beat boxing.

So I did everything I could to make sure I was on that train the next weekend. I cleaned, came when I was called and did everything Mom told me to as quickly and efficiently as I possibly could. I told Mom every chance I got how good it felt to be around Grandaddy and how much I was learning about taking a radio apart.

"Your grandfather says he asks you about church and you tell him you don't want to go."

"Oh, I would go," I said, feeling my way, "I just didn't think it would be polite to go if *he* didn't."

"Well, I think if he's willing to walk you over there and pick you up afterward like he says he is, you should get up and go to church like you've been raised to."

"Yes, ma'am. I was going to ask you if I should go whether Grandaddy goes or not. I'll go this Sunday."

She didn't say anything. Good, I thought. That must mean I'm spending the weekend in Harlem.

This time, it felt almost better than the first. It was easier than it had been the past couple of weeks to be with my grandfather, to sit in the same apartment with him and not say anything for hours. Whenever we did speak, I said whatever I knew he wanted to hear. Yes sir, I was obedient to my mother, and to Ben. Yes sir, I was doing well in school and I was definitely going to college. Yes, yes sir, I was learning to act like a man.

Sunday morning at Greater Faith Harlem Baptist Tabernacle on 161st Street turned out to be the best thing about New York. There was a thumping organ and ladies in hats with rose gardens on them. Harlem Baptist couldn't have been more different from Stratfield Methodist. There were no dragging hymns with seven verses or long droning prayers that sounded like the vowel exercises from school. It was like walking into the middle of a big, loud musical play and everyone including the audience had their part. I only wished somebody I knew was there with me, to hear the singers, and the organ and the children's choir clapping double-time. I thought about Ray Anthony and wondered if he'd ever been to New York. But then, even if he had, it was hard to picture him in anybody's church. The preacher said, "Everybody in this world is entitled to a miracle." It would be a miracle, I thought, to have Ray Anthony here with me now.

The Tabernacle Choir was singing about what a joy it was to save and be saved. How sweet, how sweet, they sang. To save and be saved. I pictured Ray Anthony out in the courtyard in his undershirt daring Bubba Graves to kick me again. Ray Anthony had saved me that day. Just like the song the Tabernacle Choir was singing. I didn't know how he felt about it, but he'd certainly come when I least expected. And saved me. Oh, how sweet, how sweet, to save and be saved.

12

Ed MacMillan wasn't on the platform when we pulled into the station. No one seemed to be in the waiting room and the ticket booth was closed. I had twenty minutes before the next bus.

He might have forgotten he ever told me I could see his office, I thought. Maybe, even if I saw him again and brought it up, he'd laugh and say he was only kidding. He hadn't acted all that friendly the last time. I'd decided it was probably better to forget about Ed MacMillan's invitation to see the world from the twenty-third floor, when I saw the cream-colored station wagon pull into the parking lot.

The closer I got to the car, the more I knew there was something different about him. His whole face was red and blotchy, like he'd been stung or had a high fever. When I got right up to the window, I was pretty sure what it was. He'd been drinking. I felt a little disappointed, but I figured it wasn't really any of my business whether he drank or not. He was smiling now, the smile from the first time.

"Nobody coming to pick you up?"

"No. I take the bus. But it doesn't matter which one. Long as I get home before midnight." I was trying to make a joke, but I couldn't tell whether he got it or not, because his smile didn't change.

"Get in."

I threw my suitcase on the backseat and jumped in front beside him. He had on his navy blue windbreaker. I wanted to tell him, "You look like a kid in that jacket." But he didn't really look like any kid I knew. He'd probably think I was saying he looked shrimpy.

The radio was on. "Soul Man" was playing. "Soul Man" was the kind of song that made nearly every part of my body want to move to it. Especially the horns. Ed MacMillan was beating his fingers against the steering wheel to the horns. I didn't say anything for a while. Then I did, because I thought I shouldn't just sit there like I was stupid or being rude to him. "Where're we going?"

He didn't answer right away. He put his thumb up to his mouth and chewed on it for a second. I thought I'd done something dumb after all by asking. Then he said, "Just driving." He looked over at me. "That okay with you?"

"Sure," I said, relieved. I also felt better that even if he had been drinking, he wasn't in a bad mood or depressed. As far as I could tell, he was driving pretty decently. He'd gone right onto the highway instead of driving into town. I liked that because it felt like neither one of us had any ties to Stratfield. What was better was that he was driving toward New York. Maybe, even though it was Sunday, I was on my way back to the city. I'd get to see what he was calling half the world from his office window on the twenty-third floor.

I opened my mouth and started breathing in and out in time to the horns. I didn't think he could hear me. Huh-huh-huh-huhhh. Huh-huh. Huh-huh-huh-huhhh. Huh-huh.

"I know you're going to be mad at me for this," he said, "but I guess I should admit it sooner rather than later."

"What's the matter?" Don't let anything spoil it, I thought. No, nothing could. Whatever it was, I was still probably on my way to 49th Street in New York. With the radio on a station that played the perfect music for traveling.

"I don't remember your name. I know it begins with a C."

"No. It doesn't. *L*. It's Louis." It didn't make sense that he wouldn't remember. It was because he'd been drinking. That was the reason. He probably forgot things when he drank. Even important things.

"Shit. That's right. Louis." He hit the steering wheel and honked the horn by mistake. "Oh c'mon. Don't look like that. I bet you don't remember mine either."

"MacMillan," I said quietly. "Ed MacMillan. Where are we going?" This time I didn't care what he thought about me asking. It was the only thing I could think of to get back at him. He reached over and grabbed my thigh, pulling me toward him.

"Move over."

I didn't. I held on to the car seat, looking straight ahead at the two white lines on the highway.

When he turned off, we were outside Stratfield. There was a string of flat-looking motels on either side of the road. He pulled up at the end of a horseshoe path outside one of them with a sign that said "Friends and Travellers."

Ed MacMillan leaned toward me.

When he walked up the path to the Friends and Traveller's office I thought, This was pretty dumb, Louis. You're not on your way to New York and if you think you and Ed MacMillan are stopping at a motel to watch TV, you're out of your mind.

I checked the clock on the dashboard. Almost six-thirty. If I didn't call Mom soon she'd have called the police by the time I did.

Ed MacMillan came back to the car a few minutes later. "Put your head down on the seat. I'm going to drive around to the other side." He sounded like we were robbing a bank, as if we'd planned it and I should know what to do.

"I want to go back," I told him.

"We will." He sounded out of breath. "I just want to stop here for a minute. Please."

I stared at him, trying to figure out the easiest way back to Stratfield. I pulled myself into a ball on my side, the top of my head against his leg. When he pulled around to park, I got dizzy. He turned off the engine and I felt his clammy palm on my cheek.

"Stay here. I'm going to open the door. Wait for a minute and then come in quickly."

Reaching across my body, he pressed the button on the glove compartment. The door fell open and he took out a small brown paper bag I figured had a bottle of whiskey in it. He patted me lightly on the back. I heard the door open and slam again.

"I have to call my mother," I said as soon as I got inside. "Then I want to go back."

Ed MacMillan pointed to the phone on his way into the bathroom. I waited for him to close the door, but he didn't. He didn't even turn on the light. I stood by the side of the bed and dialed the number.

I'd never been in a motel before. The room we were in had fake wood paneling on the walls. Somebody'd carved a whole letter in it, with a knife or a can opener, maybe. The letter was addressed to "Dear Sofia" and signed "Alan." It said, "You should know how much I love and need you, but if you ever have any doubt, this is prof. No one will ever mean as much to me as you have been." Obviously, Alan didn't believe in proofreading. And where was Sofia when he wrote it? Was she coming later when he wouldn't be there?

The dresser was cheap looking, white with gold sparkles like a kitchen countertop, and there wasn't any TV. All the motels in movies had TVs. The bed took up most of the room. It had one of those bedspreads with the little nubs all over it, like tassels except really short ones. There were more than a few cigarette burns up near the pillows.

"Mom, it's me. I'm still downtown. I had to use the men's room when I got to the station and when I came out, I'd missed the bus."

Mom asked me how many times she'd asked me not to use the men's room at the train station.

"I know, Mom. I couldn't help it. Anyway, I met this kid from school who was on the train with his mother and they're going to give me a ride home but we have to stop at their house first. They want to know if I can eat dinner with them."

Mom wanted to know who the kid was. I hadn't asked to eat at anyone's house since kindergarten.

"Michael Epstein." Michael Epstein was the kid who'd asked me in kindergarten. His family had moved since then, but I didn't know whether she'd remember or not.

Where did they live, Mom wanted to know. I had no idea where Michael Epstein lived. I made sure I told her somewhere in the school zone.

Was his mother there? Mom wanted to speak to her.

"No Mom, they're in the car." I was doing well enough to fake sounding anxious, like I was keeping Mrs. Epstein waiting out in the parking lot.

Don't stay there too late, Mom warned me. It had worked. If Ed MacMillan got back in the car and drove me back to the Stratfield station right now, I could get on the next bus and be home to tell Mom dinner at Michael Epstein's had been fine and I had to go right upstairs to work on my book report.

I went to the bathroom door. Ed MacMillan was sitting on the side of the tub in the dark with his bottle in the paper bag. The air around him smelled like whiskey and apricot candy. He was biting his nails.

"Is it alright if we go back now?"

He reached out, grabbed under my jacket for my belt buckle and pulled me toward him. He pushed his face into my stomach, his fists holding me from behind.

"We're going back. In a minute."

He pulled me in tighter, then lifted me, carried me out of the bathroom. When he dropped me onto the bed and fell on top of me, I bit my lip.

I opened my eyes to see his own lips were shiny with spit, his plaid shirt bunched and wrinkled under his wind-breaker. He pushed me over onto my stomach, pinning me down by my shoulders, his stubbly chin scratching the side of my neck.

He stopped moving suddenly like a machine that had been cut off. When I looked behind me, he was on his knees between my legs, quickly undoing his pants. His thighs were small and pale like his face and hands.

"No," I told him. "I thought we were going to—" When he jerked his underpants down, a swollen, purplish thumb of a dick with wiry hair around it pointed up toward the ceiling. Ed MacMillan fell over on me, his hands went up to my neck holding my head so that my face was crushed into the bed.

I yelled into the burned nubs on the spread. The bed shook and sank lower under me like I was being swallowed by a wave. I froze for a moment, but when Ed

MacMillan pulled back, I bucked so hard against him he lost his grip. Turning under him, I tried to sit up. He came back down over me with his hands anchored around my neck again. I couldn't breathe. I punched up at his head, into his face. Ed MacMillan looked surprised now, and angry. He hadn't looked angry till now.

He drew one of his fists back above my face, the other hand pushing down on my throat. I kept punching at him, aiming my knuckles at his eyes.

"Dammit! Sonofabitch!" he shouted. But he let go. Slowly, he crawled backwards off the bed, his belly low like he'd been shot.

"Why'd ya wanna fight me?" he whispered. "I thought we were friends. I thought you wanted . . . to be with me."

I sat up immediately, staring at him, daring him to come back. I looked through him, picturing myself on the train to New York, staring out the window at Stratfield going by. Then I heard Ed MacMillan's voice in the distance, like he was speaking to me from outside, in the parking lot.

"Well, c'mon then. We have to go."

Go on, edfuckingmacmillan. I just want to sit here. I want to sit here on the train, looking out the window, watching Stratfield disappear.

Ed MacMillan was whining like a six-year-old child. "Louis, c'mon now. Pleeeze." He wandered into the bathroom. "I must be crazy," he said. "I must be crazy." Coming back to the bed he told me, "If you don't get up, I'm going to have to leave you here. You don't want me to leave you here, do you?"

I stood up and slowly, carefully pushed my shirt back into my pants. Ed MacMillan watched me from the corner of the room. He took a swig from his bag and opened the door. "That's a good boy. C'mon now."

He told me he'd take me back to the train station. "I'll give you some money so you can take a cab home."

I wouldn't get back in his car. He sat there for a few minutes trying to bargain with me, but eventually he took one long, last drink and drove off. I was glad not to have to look at him anymore. Walking the side of the highway, I passed two exits until I saw the sign that said "Exit 34, Stratfield Railroad Station." A train was just moving off toward New York.

I hoped I'd gotten in at least one good punch, something that would show up on his head or his face for a few days at least. I hoped I'd hurt him.

There was no bus in either direction. Who knew when the next one would be. Should've taken his fucking cab money.

I put my hand up to my neck remembering how I couldn't breathe and he wouldn't let go. I'd told myself, you have to make him stop, Louis, you have to make him take his hands away.

I could hear Mom the first time she'd snatched me by the shirt collar and pulled me face to face with her after watching me fight in the courtyard.

"Why the hell didn't you kill him, Louis?" she'd demanded and actually waited for an answer. "Can you give me one good reason why you didn't kill him?"

Sunday night. Have to get home fast. Book report due tomorrow. Have to get home.

13

Mom finally won. Or at least she knew where she stood.
Ben told her he wouldn't look for a house himself for us
to move to, but if she found one and was willing to pay
half the rent on it, he'd move in. Mom pretended it was
the answer she'd been waiting for, but I knew better. I
kept waiting for her to ask him, "If I can find a house
myself, what do I need you for?" Instead, when he was
around she'd act almost grateful. It seemed to me she was
angrier with him than she'd ever been. She stopped waiting for nighttime or Saturdays to have a drink. I'd come
home from school, one of her Billie Holiday records
would be playing, and she'd be standing in the middle of
the kitchen floor with this look in her eyes that said
maybe I was home but she wasn't.

She put an ad in the *Stratfield Journal*. To make extra
money without having to leave Lorelle, she decided she'd
iron people's clothes. White people outside our neighborhood, even a couple from the other side of the city,
brought baskets spilling over with shirts, sheets, underwear. Some of them clean, some not so clean. Clean or
not, Mom worked on them for hours. When she was
exhausted, she'd prop the iron up, forget it was there,
lean against it and burn herself. She'd take ice cubes from
her drink to run back and forth over her wrist, then she'd
pound the ironing board with the iron and yell, "Shit."
Pretty soon there'd be no more ice. Then she'd just hold

the glass against the burn for a minute, close her eyes and whisper, "Jesus."

Because she was trying to save money for the house, she stopped sending me to New York on the weekends. I didn't know which was worse, boxing with Ben or worrying about running into Ed MacMillan.

I was catching hell at school. Not paying attention. Not doing homework. Most of the time I felt exhausted and wanted to go to sleep. School. Home. Everywhere. I daydreamed a lot. Mostly about Ed MacMillan. The motel. I started with the motel, then I'd go back to the beginning, then the motel again.

Every time I went back, it was different. I'd pick one sound or smell or the way something felt and go over it twenty or thirty times before I let myself move on to something else. The car door slamming. My face mashed against the bedspread nubs. Ed MacMillan's fist on my neck. Me sitting on the motel bed, imagining an express train running through his chest.

And then I'd get tired and want to stop remembering. I'd only want to sleep. But it was too late. The pictures and the sounds came whether I wanted them to or not. Then I'd get called on.

"Louis." Sometimes when I heard the teacher call my name, I didn't realize she was talking to me. For a couple of seconds, I couldn't remember where I was, what class I was in.

I had warning notices in every subject except English. In English, I had a C average. There was only a month left to the term. If I didn't pull my grades up by the end of June, I'd probably have to repeat eighth grade.

By the time Dr. Shapiro, the school psychologist, called Mom, she was popping me around for not paying attention at home either and acting what she called sullen and dogwitted.

Dr. Shapiro told Mom he wanted to do what he called "an assessment" on me, but he wanted to see her first. Mom acted like I'd been caught stealing out of teachers' pocketbooks. She told me, "Now you've got those people ready to call you a mental case. Because you're willful. Because you've decided this is a good way to keep from doing whatever I ask you to do. Well, you let them call you whatever they decide to at that school. I'll straighten you out my own way when you get home."

After her appointment, Mom told me Dr. Shapiro said he thought I was depressed and asked her what could be making a kid as bright as I was do so badly all of a sudden?

"Depressed? You're depressed?" Mom asked, slapping me in the face with the word. "Here I am trying to move four people into a respectable place to live without anybody's help. And now you've decided to be some kind of mentally ill juvenile delinquent. Let me tell you something, Louis. I just wish I had the time to be mentally ill. I wish I could afford to take a few years off and be a raving lunatic!

"You were supposed to help me," she sighed. "We were supposed to be a team." She was right, I thought. My job was easy. And something in me, either criminal or crazy, I didn't know which, was making me mess it up.

Whatever it was she thought I deserved, I was really fed up with the beatings. Every time she got near me, I'd brace myself. If she reached for something, I'd duck but when she saw me she said, "You think I'm going to hit you? What for? What good would it do? It hasn't done me any good so far." I wanted to ask her why, if she figured that out, she hadn't stopped a long time ago. To her,

I guessed, I was probably worse now than I'd ever been and if she really let herself go on me, she'd probably kill me.

I managed to pass everything, even if it was borderline. Dr. Shapiro and the principal met with Mom again and said even though I hadn't flunked, they strongly recommended that I go to this place downtown called the Burgess Treatment Center, which Mom said was really an insane asylum.

"I hope you're satisfied," she told me. "You couldn't make me look any worse than this."

Burgess was actually a day treatment center, Dr. Shapiro explained to me, which still might be an insane asylum I thought, but at least they wouldn't keep me there sharing a room with some grizzled old guy wearing a dirty straitjacket and weeping. It was state-owned so Mom wouldn't have to pay anything. Dr. Shapiro thought it was a great deal. He told me to think of it as a scholarship and laughed, which made me think maybe he was a little nuts too.

I only had to go for a few hours every day, for group therapy and for a private session with him. He wanted me to start in August so I'd get used to it, then continue in the fall while I was going to school. He'd work with the principal to arrange my schedule so I wouldn't miss anything too important while I was at Burgess in the morning.

All July I spent sitting on the stoop reading library books or taking care of Lorelle while Mom ironed. I hardly ever saw Ray Anthony and when I did, we'd kind of nod at each other, but by the time I got up the nerve to say anything, either he was already gone or I got called inside. I'd take over the ironing if Mom needed a break or got nauseous, which she sometimes did, standing over the

steam inhaling spray starch and people's stinking underwear. By August I was glad I'd have someplace to go in the
mornings, even if it was "the asylum" as Mom insisted on
calling it.

14

One side of our bungalow faced the courtyard, the center of the projects. Our back door faced the street. Across the street were houses like the ones Mom wanted so desperately to live in, all sizes, all colors, with awninged porches and neatly trimmed hedges.

Directly across from us, the Sabatinos, an Italian couple, owned a pale blue, two-family house with a front lawn framed by alternating red and white zinnias. There were zinnias on either side of the driveway leading to their front porch and zinnias in window boxes on both floors of the house. Mom decided she wanted zinnias planted in the patch of dirt outside the front of our bungalow.

"It will keep us from thinking we're in a prison," she said, "and remind us that this is only a temporary condition." She would ignore, of course, the regulation that forbade tenants to plant anything on projects property.

She went across the street one day when Mr. Sabatino was on his knees planting along the driveway and asked him if zinnias were difficult to grow. She was willing to buy soil, if it was necessary. She wanted to do whatever was necessary, she flattered him, to have her home look as attractive as the home it faced across the street.

Sal Sabatino was about fifty years old and five feet tall. He didn't speak English very well and asked after almost every sentence, "Yeah, Mrs. Stamps?" to which Mom would answer, "I follow you." He assured Mom that he would be more than happy to bring some of his special planting soil across the street and plant a couple of rows of zinnias himself, if that's what she wanted. "Are you sure this isn't nothing against the law? I never seen no other flowers over there."

"If there's a problem, it won't be yours, Mr. Sabatino. I'll do what I want with where I live."

"That's right?" he laughed. "Call me Sal. You tell me when to bring the flowers over, Mrs. Stamps, and I'll plant them myself. Not a problem." And the next Saturday morning, about an hour after Ben left for work, Mr. Sabatino was on his knees in front of our bungalow, planting zinnias.

Kids from the projects called to each other to "come look at the white man planting flowers outside Miz Stamps's apartment." Mom stood on the stoop and supervised Mr. Sabatino. "Not too close to each other, Mr. Sabatino. And not too close to the street."

After he'd finished planting, I could see neighbor women watching from their windows as Mom served Mr. Sabatino iced tea on the front stoop. The two of them sat there sipping as Mom pretended not to notice she had an audience.

That night, Mom asked Ben what he thought of the zinnias.

"Something else for you to fight with these people about?" Ben asked her. "They're not all that fond of you as it is. Why do you push it? Why do you always have to call attention to yourself?"

When Mom found an ad in the newspapers for a house just outside of town, she asked Ben if he'd drive over to see it. "Please, Ben. We could all go. Just to see. At least, let's go look at it, for god's sake." Ben said, "I've already told you. I don't have any money for a house. If you have the money for one, you go see it."

Mom didn't have the money, but she was determined to see the house. I was shocked when she announced two days later, "Louis, I want you to take care of Lorelle. Mr. Sabatino is taking me to see the house from the ad in the paper."

She came back breathless with enthusiasm. "We can't afford that one, Louis. But I got Mr. Sabatino to take me to see a few others. That's the only way we're going to do it. We have to shop. We'll never get one sitting here."

The next day at Sunday dinner, she told Ben she'd gone to see the house, in spite of him. When he asked her how she got there, she said simply, "The man across the street drove me."

Ben took a swallow of water and slowly put the glass back on the table. "You got that old man driving you around to see houses now?"

As he leaned toward Mom, his voice got even softer. "You're really something, aren't you? You'd do anything to get your precious house. Wouldn't you?"

"Watch your mouth, Ben. You watch your damn mouth. I don't care what you say in private, but you watch your mouth in front of my children."

"I should watch my mouth?" He pushed away from the table and started to stand. "You know what you are?" He flipped his full plate onto the floor. "You're garbage."

He'd barely gotten the word out of his mouth. I lunged at him before he could stand. I aimed at his head, his stomach. I punched, spat, kicked, as hard and as fast as I could, slipping and skidding in mashed potatoes and corn.

For the first time, Ben ducked and dodged to protect himself. It was only for an instant, but I recognized it when it happened. In the next moment, though, he punched me in the stomach with enough force to go through me to the other side. I doubled over, then fell back. My shoulder smashed against the cinderblock wall and I slumped to the floor in pain.

Ben was winded. I'd never done that before. In all the Sundays of boxing, I'd never even managed to land a punch. He didn't come after me. He stared at me like he was trying to keep himself from coming over and killing me. Mom stood between us in front of him begging, "Please. Ben. No."

"I don't care what he does," I gasped. "I hate him."

"And you know what, you little bastard? I hate you too." With that, he was gone. We didn't see him again until Monday evening.

It was the last of the Sunday boxing matches. Till the Sunday he died.

15

I was supposed to take the bus every day to Burgess alone, but that first morning Mom and Lorelle went with me in a cab. Mom wanted to see for herself what it looked like and she thought it would look better for her to be seen driving up in a taxi instead of walking from the bus stop.

Burgess was a big, brown two-story house with a wrap-around porch and a driveway. This surprised me because for a whole month I'd imagined a redbrick building with bars on the windows hidden from the street by mile-high hedges.

No one was on the porch, but there was a face at one of the windows watching us. Mom told the cab to wait. A woman with a pink velvet bow in her hair and lipstick covering her teeth met us at the door and asked us to step into the hallway. I thought she might be one of the friendlier patients but she said, "I'm Vera Stein, the receptionist. Dr. Shapiro told me Louis was coming." She was blocking the doorway on purpose so Mom couldn't get any farther into the building.

"Hello, Louis."

As nervous as I was, I was dying to tell her to run her tongue over her teeth and clean up some of that lipstick. Mom stopped trying to see around Vera Stein and said to me, "You call me if there's any problem." As mean as she'd been about me going to this place, I could hear she was scared to leave me there. Lorelle asked, "Mom, can't I stay with Louis?" but Mom pulled her back. "Shhh. Louis will be home later." The moment they turned away, I heard Dr. Shapiro's voice at the top of the stairs behind Vera Stein.

"Come on in, Louis. Welcome."

I didn't understand why he'd told me to get there at nine since group therapy wasn't until ten. I had to sit, waiting in what they called the community room, watching the other patients drink juice and drop doughnut crumbs over everything. From the conversations around me, I found out that day treatment meant most of them had been in a hospital before coming to Burgess. Now they were living on their own, but spending a good part of the day at the center.

Lucille, the woman whose face I'd seen at the window, was a patient. Anytime she thought she heard a noise outside, she ran over and peeked from behind the curtain. Then, depending on what she saw, she'd call out to whoever was around, "It's alright! It's only the mailman!" Or, "There's somebody walking by, but they're not gonna come in!" I don't think it mattered to her whether anyone heard her or not, it was something she had to do for herself. She was the only one of the patients who spoke to me the first day. She had a very loud conversation in the front hallway during which she asked Vera what my name was. Vera said, "Why don't you go over and introduce yourself, Lucille?" To which Lucille answered, "Because I already know his name is Louis." I was sitting just a few feet away from them in the community room. Sure enough, Lucille came right in and practically shouted at me, "Is your name Louis? Your name is Louis, right? I heard them call you Louis."

Lucille was white, I was pretty sure of it, but her skin was more of a beige color. It wasn't a black person's or

Puerto Rican beige. It was a beige that looked like she could use some vitamins or maybe a lot more vegetables in her diet. Lucille had dark, curly uncombed-looking hair that had egg or cereal or something in it, the same thing she had around the corners of her mouth. She was wearing a red sweater even though it had to be about eighty-five degrees outside and a plaid skirt that reached almost to her ankles. It was hard to tell for sure, but I guessed she was around twenty-five. Thirty, at the most.

I told her, "Yes, that's right. My name is Louis."

At about twenty minutes to ten, Vera came into the community room to tell me that everyone was expected to help clean the kitchen area in the morning after juice and doughnuts, whether they ate or not. Anxious not to get off on the wrong foot, I ran in, grabbed a sponge and started washing the other patients' glasses. Lucille picked up a towel and dried them as I gave them to her. I asked her to wait until I'd had a chance to rinse them all. Even though she said, "Yes, Louis," in that same loud voice, she took the very next soapy glass from the drain and I wasn't about to ask her again. Besides, by then I'd seen about a dozen other people wandering around who'd used those glasses and none of them had volunteered to help either one of us. I saw Vera ask one huge man with some pretty nasty stains on the back of his pants if he'd wipe off the table where the doughnuts had been served. He swept the crumbs into the palm of his hand and then threw them on the floor. A black woman sat in the corner of the kitchen mumbling about how no dirty-assed white woman was gonna make her do no damn housework if she didn't want to, hell, she'd had enough of that to last her a whole damn lifetime. Given who else was around, who cared whether Lucille waited for me to rinse the glasses?

"Group," as Dr. Shapiro called it, had only about half the people I'd seen during juice and doughnut time and Lucille was one of them. Dr. Shapiro and a young, blond woman named Sarah were supposed to be the group leaders except Sarah never said anything after she introduced herself to me. She sat next to Dr. Shapiro in the circle and took notes. When she wasn't taking notes, she was twirling her ponytail with her pencil and flicking it back over her shoulder. It was the kind of habit someone should've told her was definitely too irritating to keep doing in front of mental patients.

In Group, when I had to introduce myself, Lucille said, "Now we have a kid in here," and I thought, I am. I'm the only kid. Everyone's older than I am and they're crazier too. When Dr. Shapiro asked me in front of everyone if I had any thoughts about what Lucille said, I just muttered, "No. I don't have any thoughts about it. I guess it's true. I guess I am the youngest." I wanted to sound calm. All of the others were fidgeting and smoking and getting up to walk around the room. I measured the distance from where I sitting to the door, thinking if anyone did anything dangerous, it wasn't that far to run.

When it was her turn, Lucille talked about her new apartment, how she liked the colors of the walls and the floor and the only chair she had, which she let her dog Trisket sit in. Group was almost over before I figured out that Trisket was a stuffed animal. I was thinking about how interesting it all was and what a good psychologist Dr. Shapiro seemed to be when I remembered that I was nutso too or I wouldn't have been there.

After Group, while I was waiting to see Dr. Shapiro for what he called "our private," there was snacktime. I was too nervous to have an appetite and even if I had, watching the other patients eat would have ruined it. They weren't any better with saltines than they'd been with doughnuts. Most of them either ate like it would be their last meal, gulping and shoveling the crackers in, or they mashed them them into their pockets to save for later. Lucille came up and offered me some of hers, which she'd crumbled into small pieces.

"Aren't you going to have snacktime, Louis?"

I was afraid to upset her. As gently as I could, I told her I wasn't hungry. She looked disappointed and shuffled off to eat her saltine crumbs alone, staring out the front window. When Vera came in and announced snacktime was over, though, Lucille came back and shouted, "Let's clean up, Louis," and once again, we went to the sink together and washed and dried everyone else's glasses.

During "our private," I told Dr. Shapiro about both the thinking and the remembering I'd done during Group. He smiled and said that was good and that he had a feeling I'd be doing both. I asked him if it was necessary for me to come every day. What I really wanted to know was if he thought I was as much of a lunatic as everybody else there. I couldn't tell if he understood what I was really asking. But he answered, "Yes."

Mom asked when I got home, "You tell those people all our business?"

"No," I told her. "I didn't say hardly anything at all."

"Don't con me, Louis," she said. "I've had enough conning to last me a lifetime. That's what makes *me* crazy. Con artists and liars."

Going to Burgess every day didn't stop me from feeling exhausted all the time. Actually, I thought it might be getting worse. When I got home, I'd sneak a nap. Mom asked me, "What good does it do for you to spend half the day at that asylum if you still come back here and lie around like a junkie?"

The junkie thing must have been on her mind for a while. I didn't actually get what she was talking about until one night when I'd fallen asleep in my clothes and left the light on. It was a little after one in the morning when she opened the door to my room and woke me up. She just stared at me questioningly and left. I got up and started to get undressed when she came back with Ben. They took the lampshade off my night table light and made me hold out my arms.

Mom was the one who'd told me what a junkie was when she told me about Billie Holiday. I pretended I was Billie and she and Ben were cops when she was holding my arm up to the light. I'd never thought about *me* being a junkie before. When had Mom started to think about it?

I went to sleep remembering how Miss Odessa told Mom once the reason Ray Anthony Robinson wore dark glasses at night was because *he* was a junkie. "You better believe it," she'd said, as though Mom's believing it would make it the truth.

In my dream, Ray Anthony and I were on the train to New York, wearing hats with little brims like the one Ray Anthony'd worn to Delilah Buggman's party. We also had on dark glasses, very dark with square black frames.

Sitting very close to each other, almost touching, but not quite, both of us were singing, softly. Miss Odessa and Mom were in the seat behind us. Miss Odessa told her it was a shame what I'd become, hanging around with Ray Anthony.

"Hush," Mom hissed between her teeth. "You don't know what you're talking about."

Up ahead of them, I laughed, pushing my dark glasses back farther up on my nose and pulling the brim of my hat lower to meet them. Ray Anthony and I were singing "I Get a Kick Out of You." Both of us sounded exactly like Billie Holiday.

There were days when it didn't feel like it was really me going to Burgess. It was more like me taking my body there, watching it walk around, then bringing it home again. Every day, Lucille would wait for me at the window and by the end of the second week, she'd be out on the porch when I came up the driveway. Even when she was having a bad day, we washed the dishes together. There were quite a few bad days, though, and by the end of the month a lot of Burgess's glasses had to be replaced.

I still never said much in Group. I figured eventually Dr. Shapiro would realize that it wasn't making me any better to sit there and watch the rest of the patients fidget and mumble and tear up tissues. Even Lucille got upset and whined to Dr. Shapiro in front of everybody, "Why does Louis have to come to Group? He never says anything. He just stares at me like I'm insane or something."

The more excited the patients in Group got, the calmer Dr. Shapiro became. He'd ask them, "Are you taking your medication?" I didn't understand how he didn't know. Sarah gave everybody their medication at breakfast. Even if a patient didn't answer, Sarah wouldn't speak up and say that she knew they took it, because she'd given it to them. Every once in a while, some guy would be going off at the top of his lungs about something ridiculous and Dr. Shapiro would be asking him in this low voice if he took his pill. I'd be tempted to butt in and say, "Cut the bullshit, why don't you? You know Sarah gave it to him. It isn't working. He's still a lunatic, that's the problem! Get him out of here before he hurts somebody!"

Dr. Shapiro knew what he was doing, though. Just when I started measuring how fast I could get to the door again, he'd calm the nut down, speaking practically under his breath, but firmly as though he was taming a lion without a whip.

When I saw him alone, Dr. Shapiro would say, "Give yourself permission, Louis, to say as much or as little as you want to." I didn't mind talking about Ben. Dr. Shapiro was really interested in the details of the Sunday boxing matches. I told him I thought it was a chance for Ben to hit me like he'd always wanted to, except that now Mom had given him permission.

When Dr. Shapiro pushed me for details about Mom, I used his "say as little or as much" policy. I kept it on the "little" side. Despite what he said about not forcing me, Dr. Shapiro did ask one day, "When do you think you'll feel comfortable enough to say more about your mom?"

I told him what I thought was all anyone needed to know. "Mom and I were supposed to be a team and I let her down. She's pretty damn mad about it. I don't know if she'll ever stop being mad."

I knew I'd never tell anyone about Ed MacMillan and I wondered if I'd ever tell Dr. Shapiro about Ray Anthony. The answer, I was pretty sure, was no. It didn't feel necessary to tell anyone about Ray Anthony. Most of what I knew about him or thought about him anyway, I'd made up. If I started talking about someone who was definitely real, but also made up, I knew Dr. Shapiro would add on about five more years to the time he thought I should be at Burgess.

•   •   •

It was a Thursday when Dr. Shapiro told us in Group, "Visitors are coming tomorrow and the schedule will be a little different, but nothing we can't all handle if we work together."

I knew he was putting it that way because anytime anything was the least bit different at Burgess, the patients pouted and slammed around all day. Some of them cried about hating to have to be there because people were so inconsiderate. Vera once got into a fight with the Cursing Colored Woman because she bought fake Oreos for snacktime. The Cursing Colored Woman told Vera, "Y'all take the damn taxpayers' money and stick it up your asses, insteada takin' care of the damn taxpayers like you say you're gonna. Don't you think we know the difference between real cookies and these shittin' fake ones?" The Cursing Colored Woman was the loudest when anything was different, but all the patients weirded out in their own way.

In our private, I asked Dr. Shapiro about the visitors. He leaned over his desk and scratched his scalp with both hands so that dandruff fell out. He brushed it off the side of the desk and said, "Louis, because I think you're a very mature young man, I'm going to share this with you."

"Yeah?" I said, wondering if what he was really saying now was that I was definitely a lot less insane than the others. Or maybe he could tell I was getting better.

"The *Stratfield Journal* is coming tomorrow to do a story on Burgess. We tried to get them to come on Saturday when the patients aren't here, but they said no. We can't close the center just so the paper can get a story, but we also want to protect the patients' privacy. So we're going to arrange it so that the patients stay in the Group Room, at least while they're taking pictures."

"Why?" I wanted to know. "Wouldn't it be better if the pictures showed that Burgess had some patients in it?" The building itself looked like just what it was, an old falling-down house, nothing too pretty to look at, nothing I could see worth writing about.

Dr. Shapiro told me other patients might not want their picture taken and that the center had to do what was best for everyone. He said for some of them it would be as if a stranger came into their house and started taking pictures and couldn't I understand how they'd be upset by that?

"I guess you're right," I told him. "I never had to think about my picture being taken in an asylum before."

Dr. Shapiro reminded me that Burgess wasn't an asylum, and I didn't argue with him. But I knew other people would be thinking it was an asylum. A nuthouse. Wasn't that going to be the point of the story?

The next morning I pulled out my blue dress shirt and a pair of black pants I usually only wore to church.

"Where do you think you're going in those pants?" Mom asked me. "You getting dressed up to go to that place, now? You must be really losing your mind."

I changed the pants, but I still got away with wearing the shirt.

After Group, Dr. Shapiro made an announcement that we should all stay in the room and Vera was going to bring in some cookies and juice for snacktime. The Cursing Colored Woman insisted she wanted tea. "Why the hell can't I have a cup of nice hot tea?!" she demanded, even though the Group Room was like an oven. Dr. Shapiro asked her, "Gloria, why don't you have some juice now and get your cup of tea a little later, maybe after lunch?"

The Cursing Colored Woman started up and when she did I headed for the door. Sarah stopped in the middle of twirling her hair and called out, "Louis, where are you going?"

"To the men's room."

Dr. Shapiro was really tense by now. "Can't you wait, Louis?"

"No. I can't."

He came to the door where I was standing and looked out into the hallway. There wasn't anyone there, but I could hear Vera's voice upstairs on the second floor.

"Go ahead," Dr. Shapiro whispered, rubbing the back of his neck with both hands. When he'd closed the door to the Group Room, I went to the bottom of the stairs and listened. Vera was showing the photographers the upstairs offices. They'd be down soon. When I heard them coming, I ran into the kitchen and waited.

"Now the Group Room, as I told you, is being used right now," I could hear Vera telling them, coming downstairs. "But to the left here is the kitchen—" She stopped.

"L—" she started again, then caught herself. "What are you doing in here?" She was smiling, but underneath the smile I could hear, "I could twist your ears off your lousy little head, Louis!"

I smiled myself, at all of them. There was a woman reporter who immediately started writing something and a photographer who looked as if he didn't know what he should do next. I felt sorry for Vera. Her whole body was twitching. I'd never seen anybody have a stroke before, but I was pretty sure it couldn't be too different from what was going on with her.

"Hi," I said to all of them. "I'm Louis." Then to Vera, "I'm fixing a cup of tea for—" I stopped myself. It wouldn't be fair to say any of the other patients' names. "I'm going to fix myself a cup of tea."

Continuing to smile at the photographer, I was saying to him, "Go on. Take it. Take a picture. I'm Louis Bowman. Son of Jeanette Stamps. Grandson of Donald Emmanuel Suggs. I'm the youngest one in here. I'm thirteen years old. And shittin' crazy, as Gloria, The Cursing Colored Woman would say. I'm shittin' crazy." I wanted Mom to see that picture on the front page with my name under it. At least she couldn't say I hadn't worn one of my best shirts.

Vera ran for Dr. Shapiro. By the time he got to the kitchen, I had volunteered several details about Burgess I thought would make a good story, without giving any of the patients' names, of course, but I still didn't get my picture taken. Dr. Shapiro asked me in our private what I'd hoped to accomplish by what I'd done. I told him, "I wanted to get my picture in the newspaper. There might be some other kids out there who are just as crazy as I am. They'd know they weren't the only ones."

At the end of the last week in August, Dr. Shapiro told me that he wanted me to know before he announced it in Group, he wouldn't be working at Burgess anymore. He also wouldn't be at school in September. He said he had a new job, but I could tell he wasn't going to say anything about it. He didn't usually say anything about himself. He'd told me before we weren't there to talk about him.

"But from now on," he said, "your therapist will be Dr. Davis. Although I'll miss talking to you, I know you're going to like her a lot. Unfortunately, you'll have a bit of a break because she won't be here until the second week of September."

At first, I just looked at him for a long time. I had to look away, though, to stop myself from crying. Then I wanted to yell like the other crazies did. I wanted to curse at him and ask him, "Why the hell did you make me come to this nuthouse if you knew you were going to leave me here?" I wasn't going to tell anything to this Dr. Davis. Since they decided I was insane, I could act insane. I could act as nuts as anybody in there and who would stop me? Like Mom told me all the time, "There isn't any white man gonna save you. You keep walking where they tell you to walk, you'll be lost before you know it."

16

The day I came home from Burgess and saw Ray Anthony in the parking lot, I grabbed my chance to talk to him, really talk to him for as long as he'd let me.

"Ray Anthony!" I yelled, running to him, "You working this summer? I haven't seen you."

"Yeah," he answered, as though he was used to us having conversations, as though he wasn't at all surprised I was asking. "I got me my same job I always had."

"What's that?" I tried to sound casual like maybe he'd told me a long time ago, but I'd forgotten.

"At the Sunoco station. End of Blackburn Avenue."

"Oh, right," I said. "What do you do?" That was real stupid, I thought. What does anybody do who works at a gas station?

"Mostly, fix engines. Sometime I gotta pump some gas. But what he hired me for is that I can fix any kinda engine. Any kind."

His confidence made me feel proud.

"Where you comin' from?" I could hardly believe he was asking. I panicked, not wanting to lie to him.

"This place," I started. "It's called Burgess. I go every day." Then it began to pour out of me like I'd been waiting for weeks to tell him. I didn't think about being ashamed or that he'd laugh or tell anyone else. It seemed right that he should know. In my mind, Ray Anthony should know anything he wanted to about me. Except about Ed MacMillan.

Even so, as I told him about how I hadn't been doing that well in school, that Dr. Shapiro suggested Burgess and how upset Mom had been upset about it, I stared at the corner of his shoulder because I couldn't quite look in his eyes. Standing there in the parking lot, I told him as much as I could as quickly as I could, not having any idea what would come next, just knowing I couldn't stop. When I finished, or at least slowed down because I couldn't think of anything else to say, Ray Anthony reached into his back pocket and took out a stick of spearmint gum. He slowly ripped it in half, frowning at it like it took all his concentration.

"You want half?"

I took the piece he held out to me and waited for him to unwrap his half so we could start to chew together, at the same time.

Finally he said, "I know Burgess. Everybody know Burgess. Ain't you too young to be in a place like that?"

"I'm the youngest." I looked up at him. I'd never felt as young as I did at that moment. Burgess didn't matter. I wanted to be old enough for Ray Anthony to take me seriously.

"You know," he started, and I could tell he wasn't sure how to say it, "you can't let nobody tell you you crazy. Just cause you ain't out here doin' what everybody else is doin.' That don't make you crazy."

I nodded. "I know." And I remembered days I was sure I *was* crazy. I was glad Ray Anthony didn't think so, though.

"They don't wire nothin' to your head, do they?"

I laughed. "You mean, shock treatment? No. They don't do that to anybody there."

Ray Anthony laughed too. He looked a little embarrassed. "I was just makin' sure."

He shook his head slowly from side to side. Something about the way he did it reminded me of Grandaddy. It was as if he was staring into a pool that only he could see, reflecting back on all the years he'd already lived, all the experiences he'd already had.

"Least you ain't locked up nowhere."

"Yeah," I agreed with him, wishing I could see into his pool of memories.

"You do whatever they tell you to. Just so it don't cross their minds to lock you up somewhere."

"I do," I told him. "I always do what they tell me to."

Suddenly Ray Anthony spat his gum out on the ground between us. He looked at me sharply.

"You know, Burgess ain't all that far from the garage. Them people get too much for ya, I'll come over there with the old man's truck and run it through the place a couple times." He laughed in this voice that sounded like he was only half joking and I was reminded of why people could think he was dangerous. But when he started to walk away from me out of the parking lot, I wanted to follow him. I wanted to be with him, at the garage or wherever he was going.

"Ray Anthony!" He turned back, but I didn't have the guts to ask if I could go with him. There wasn't anything else I could say to keep him there with me. "I'll see ya."

The only thing I wanted more than to go with him was to know that he really would drive up to Burgess one day. He wouldn't have to run through it a couple of times like he said. He'd just have to get as far as the front of the building. I'd be waiting on the porch.

As he walked out of the parking lot, he reached into his back pocket for another stick of gum. I could hear the thumping of the organ and the choir of Greater Faith Tabernacle. I could hear the preacher saying, "Everybody in this world is entitled to a miracle."

I'll be waiting, I thought. I'll watch for you every day.

17

September. Mom was panicking. She wasn't making enough money to save anything for the new house and she was anxiously trying to figure out what else to do. She began saying things now I knew she didn't mean, like how it was a damn shame she had me around her neck since I wasn't doing anything but flunking school and going to the nuthouse. "I'll be glad," she told me, "when you get old enough for me to pack your bags and put them out there on the stoop."

She was threatening to put Ben's bags on the stoop now too so it made me feel a little better. Ben snickered at her. "I don't need you to pack for me. I know how to pack." But he never did.

At school, my average from eighth grade put me in a class with kids I'd avoided my whole life. Guys who'd already beat me up, guys who were waiting to. Girls who sucked their teeth constantly at the teacher, at each other, at everyone else in the room. As if sucking their teeth took the place of English. This was the class I'd put myself in. It was nobody's fault but my own.

For the two weeks after Dr. Shapiro left Burgess, Sarah took over Group and I didn't have any private sessions. I decided Sarah was something between a student and an actual psychologist. We sat in the room for an hour while she practically begged the nuts to sit down and control themselves. I made this joke with myself that if she had any sense at all, she'd triple their medication. Nobody would know except her. She could sit in the Group Room twirling her hair, watching them drool and nod.

By the Monday Dr. Davis was supposed to start, I had pretty much convinced myself to have an open mind about her. I missed talking to someone about Mom and Ben, especially since things seemed to be getting worse. I hadn't told Dr. Shapiro everything, but what I did say somehow made me feel better. If I could stand this new person at all, at least I'd have someone to tell whatever I chose to tell them. I knew she had to lead Group first, so that would give me a chance to see how bad or good she was at being a therapist with the loons before I had her for our private.

I imagined that Dr. Davis would be everything Dr. Shapiro was not. Tall and blow-away thin, because Dr. Shapiro was thick looking, not fat, but solid like he ate steak and baked potatoes with a couple of glasses of wine every night. Dr. Davis, I had decided, was spindly and either very old or even younger than Sarah. Just graduated or ready to retire. Either way, she didn't have a family and would probably always be snooping around the patients' food like I saw Sarah doing, looking for something to eat. She and Sarah would never be able to control the patients in Group. I'd still be respectful, no matter how badly I thought they were doing their jobs, but the rest of the nuts would eat poor Dr. Davis and mealy-mouthed Sarah alive.

When I got to Burgess on the Monday morning Dr. Davis arrived, Lucille was waiting on the porch. When she saw me, she started jumping up and down, clapping her hands like a kid at Christmas. "She's here! The new doctor is here! Wait till you see her! You're gonna die!" That's all she would say.

It was enough to send me through the building on a search. I ran past Vera at the front desk upstairs to the second floor. The door to Dr. Shapiro's office, which now belonged to Dr. Davis was open, but she wasn't in it. I ran back down, asked Vera where she was. She said Dr. Davis was in a meeting. I'd have to wait until after breakfast to see her at Group.

I left some of the breakfast glasses in the drain without washing them which made Lucille very upset. I ran back downstairs, expecting that Dr. Davis would be early the first time at least, instead of coming in a couple minutes late like Dr. Shapiro always did. Sarah announced that Dr. Davis was still in a meeting, but would be there soon. With her head cocked to the side and her eyes closed, Lucille repeated, "Wait till you see her, Louis. You're gonna die!"

When I finally did see her, I knew why Lucille was so excited. Dr. Davis sailed into the group room like a big cocoa-colored ship, with curled blue hair and red-framed glasses. There wasn't one thing about the way she looked that was what I'd imagined. And from the way they suddenly stopped pacing and tearing tissues, I could tell the other patients were surprised too. "Wha'd I tell ya?!" Lucille yelled across the room at me.

Dr. Davis sat next to Sarah and put her pocketbook on the floor. I couldn't tell how old she was, definitely older than my mother, but not as old as Grandaddy. She didn't have any wrinkles at all, maybe because she was so big. She wasn't fat from the waist down, but she did have a bigger chest than any woman I could think of at that moment. The blue hair was what made her look old. She should have dyed it any other color but old-lady blue, I thought. Mostly, though, I couldn't get over Dr. Davis being black.

"I'd like to know who everyone is," she said, and she

reminded me of Mom because her voice was so clear and you could hear "Don't you dare mess with me" in every word. She also had a slight accent, which made her voice sound musical, like the organ chimes at Greater Faith Tabernacle. "But I want everyone to sit down first so that we can all see each other when we speak."

Probably Dr. Shapiro had started out trying to get everybody to sit down like they were sane when he first started. I had no way of knowing. But it was certainly too late now. Even Sarah looked at Dr. Davis as if to say, "It's a nice thought, lady. But it's never going to happen."

The patients watched her as if, of course, she was the one who was a loon for even asking. Dr. Davis smiled at them and shrugged. "We won't be able to begin until everyone sits down." Maybe what they heard in her voice was "Even if I am bonkers, it's what I want and I'm determined to get it." Or maybe it was because they were curious to see what would happen if they all sat down around the big brown ship with the blue hair. Slowly they drifted over like sleepwalkers being drawn into the middle of the room. Sarah looked impressed. Lucille shouted across the circle to me, "Wha'd I tell ya, Louis?! Couldn't ya just die?!"

Before I had time to worry about what I was or wasn't going to say to her, Dr. Davis told me to make sure the door was closed. She pulled open one of the drawers at the side of her desk and took out a red plaid-patterned thermos and a small stack of paper cups.

"You like ginger ale?"

"Yes, ma'am."

She poured, and held one of the cups out toward me. "Cold enough? Or do you need some ice from the kitchen?"

The accent was West Indian. Mom said West Indians didn't have any use for American black people, so I wouldn't mention it to her when I told her about Dr. Davis.

"No ma'am. It's fine, thank you."

While we drank, she reached for a small gold elephant sitting in the corner of her desk. She lit a cone of incense sitting in a hole in the middle of the elephant's back. Then she stood.

"I know you told me your name in group, but it doesn't feel like we've really met each other. I'm Dr. Eleanor Davis."

We shook hands. "I'm Louis Bowman."

The first few days of seeing Dr. Davis alone were like visiting an older aunt I didn't know I had. No matter how uneasy I might have felt, she acted as if I was visiting her at home and there wasn't any reason why we both shouldn't feel as comfortable as she did. We always had a cup of ginger ale and she always burned her incense. She put on pink hand cream that smelled like roses while she asked me about my mother. Or she told me, "Blue, Louis, is your color. Take good care of that shirt you have on. It shows off how handsome you are." Like Dr. Shapiro, she told me I didn't have to tell her anything I didn't want to. "Don't feel like talking?" she'd ask. "Sit and rest for a few minutes. If something comes, fine. If not, we'll be seeing each other plenty. And we'll be friends."

She must've seen something in my face that made her add, "I am sure that we will."

18

I didn't think I'd told Dr. Davis very much, considering how much there was to tell. By the end of October, I knew I could never tell anybody all of it. Unlike Dr. Shapiro, Dr. Davis didn't mind talking about herself, especially about being a girl in Jamaica. She told me, "I grew up feeling like a unicorn in my parents' front yard, and that suited me really. But no one else seemed very pleased with me for a very long time. Sometimes you remind me of myself, Louis Bowman."

She took off her glasses, placed them in the middle of her desk and ran her finger down the bridge of her nose as she spoke gently to me. "The circumstances could not be more different, the places, the people. But the feelings, the feelings I remember well."

Mom was still taking in ironing, but now she'd also gone back to cleaning offices on Saturdays. She told me, "It's money, Louis. I close my eyes, think about my check and keep moving." I took care of Lorelle and ironed anything of her customers' Mom thought I couldn't ruin. Jeans, handkerchiefs, underwear. As exhausted as she looked, she was never too tired to battle with Ben. She didn't seem to be afraid he'd put her in the hospital like several other men in the projects had done to their wives. It was worse though now, because I was always jumping in. Even when I knew she'd started it, I couldn't stand to see him fight her back. I'd get between them and try to get in a few good punches. As soon as he started to fight me and not her, Mom would cry and beg him to stop. I was glad not to be afraid of him anymore. I fought him without thinking he could hurt me. It didn't matter anymore.

When he wasn't around, Mom would say, "Louis, you're going to make him murder you if you don't stop. I can take care of myself, but what am I going to do if he murders you?"

The Saturday night before my fourteenth birthday, Mom was cooking spaghetti, Ben was upstairs and Lorelle and I were watching television. Mom had called from her office cleaning job and told me to make sure Lorelle took her bath and put on her pajamas. She'd also asked me if I'd ironed the sheets and pillowcases Mrs. Ippolito had put in her basket that week and I told her I had. I decided to wait until she got home to tell her I'd scorched one of the pillowcases. She found it before I got the chance.

"Why do you have to be such a damn sneak? Why couldn't you act like a man for once? Didn't you think I was gonna find it, you little sneak?"

"I was gonna tell you, Mom. I was gonna—"

"You're a liar. On top of everything else, you're a liar too."

I sat staring at the television, trying, in my mind, to make Mom shut up, trying to make her stop calling me a sneak, a liar, wishing I'd taken the pillowcase outside and thrown it away.

Ben came downstairs. Now it would get worse. She'd drag him into it when it was none of his business. Tonight, he was the good one. I was the sneak, the liar.

"Turn the news on. Can you do that, at least? It's time for the news." A second ago she hadn't known or cared what was on television. Now, Ben wanted to watch the news. So it was Louis, turn on the news.

I hesitated. You want the news, here's some news, you can turn it on yourself.

Lorelle said, "I'll do it," heading toward the television.

"Oh no, you won't! Sit down!"

Lorelle jumped back onto the couch.

"Louis, what the hell is taking you so long?"

On top of everything else you sneak why do you have to be such a liarsneakliarsneakliar

I knew I was moving slowly. I couldn't go any faster. It was her fault. The louder she got, the slower I moved. Liarsneakliarsneakliar.

"Can't move any faster than that?"

I clicked the channel once.

"I bet I can make you move faster, you liar. I'll make you move—I'll make you—"

God. I hurt. What had she done to me? I was afraid to turn around. She was still behind me. Screaming. Sorry. Sorry. I could smell her. Scotch. And sweat. Screaming sorry.

19

"Look what you made me do!" Mom moaned, her voice edged with panic. I stared down at the long cooking fork she'd dropped after she jabbed it into me. "Ben, help me. Should we take him to the hospital?"

If I didn't know better, I'd have thought he didn't hear her. Finally, he said, "Put Lorelle to bed," and to me, "Louis, go upstairs to the bathroom." We filed up the stairs, Lorelle, Mom, me and Ben, splitting in separate directions at the top.

I stopped in front of the bathroom door, dazed, waiting to be told what to do next.

"Go in, and take down your pants," Ben said. "See if you're bleeding."

I went in, closed the door, and began to undress. My baggy corduroy pants were sticking to my thighs. I knew before I looked what the answer was.

"Well?" Mom asked.

I quickly locked the door. "Yes. I'm bleeding."

"For god's sake, Louis. Open the door and let me in. I want to see how bad it is."

I didn't answer.

"What do we do?" I heard her ask Ben.

There was a moment of silence. I turned my back to the sink and looked over my shoulder to the medicine chest mirror above it. I could only see as far down as the middle of my back. Where she'd jabbed me with the fork was lower, closer to my butt.

"Open the door," Ben was telling me. "If you lose too much blood, you'll have to go to the hospital."

I looked at the door, imagining the two of them out in the hall, staring from the other side. The only thing that could make this worse would be going to the hospital and having a lot of strangers look at me naked. I pictured lying on a metal table under a spotlight, with about a dozen doctors in surgical masks, all examining my butt at the same time. I pulled up my pants, unlocked the door and opened it.

"I am bleeding, but not much."

"Let me see." Mom pushed into the bathroom.

"No."

"Then Ben, you look at it, would you please?" she wailed. Ben didn't move. "Ben, *please.*"

Ben and Mom changed places, as I stood in the middle, holding my pants up with both hands, nauseous. My butt continued to sting. I looked past Mom, standing in the hallway again. Lorelle was behind her, clutching her pillow, whimpering. I closed the bathroom door.

Ben sat on the side of the tub, waiting. "I don't think it's bad," I told him.

"Let me see," he said quietly. My stomach clutched at having to take my pants down in front of him, but it didn't seem like I had a lot of choices. While he ran some warm water in the tub, I stared down at my underwear, soaked with blood.

Ben turned me around and blotted with a washcloth until he could see how bad the wound was. But he didn't tell me what he thought. He stepped away from the tub and ordered me to get in.

As I lifted my leg slowly, Mom suddenly pushed the door open. I wanted to sit quickly, but it hurt too much. I covered my crotch with both hands.

"Sit with your back to the faucet," Ben said calmly. Mom rocked back and forth on the toilet crying. "Why did you make me do this? Why?!"

She came over to the tub. I leaned away and closed my eyes, afraid of what she'd do next. Reaching into the water, she squeezed my hand. "Don't ever tell your grandfather. He'll put me in jail. He'll take you away from me." I nodded, my eyes still closed, my head against the bathroom wall. "You've got to promise me, Louis, you won't tell. Not just him. Anyone." I wanted to hit her. Instead, I promised. She let go of my hand and went back to sit on the toilet.

When she asked Ben, "Has the bleeding stopped?" he didn't answer. He turned the faucets on harder and told me, "Stay under the water." Then he started out of the bathroom. I stared down at the cloudy, red water, wondering how long it would take.

"We won't have to take him to the hospital, will we?"

Ben was already in the hallway when he told her, "You're gonna kill somebody before it's all over."

"Dr. Davis," I wanted to say on Monday while she was circling her palms with hand cream, "my mother put two little holes in me Saturday night because I scorched a pillowcase and didn't change the channel fast enough. Do you want to see them?" But I didn't. I didn't pull up my shirt, push my pants down and peel back the bandage for her like I daydreamed I would, lying in bed on Sunday. I didn't wince from how sore it was when I sat next to her in Group or across from her in our private. I kept my promise to Mom.

Dr. Davis knew something had happened to me anyway. She waited till Wednesday. Then she dropped the "you can tell me as little or as much as you want" routine.

"You've got something important on your mind, Louis? I would hope you'd trust me enough to talk about it." She put both creamed palms on her desk and leaned across it. "But I won't press you."

She often said things I didn't usually hear people say, like "I won't press you." Sometimes I'd take something she'd said and use it in school like I'd been saying it for years. "I won't press you." That was a good one.

I liked that she knew something important had happened whether I told her or not. But no, Dr. Davis, I thought, don't press me.

That Friday was my birthday. Dr. Davis announced it in Group. Lucille started singing so loud and off-key, I started laughing. No one else was singing, not even Sarah or Dr. Davis who'd brought it up in the first place, so it was pretty embarrassing. Lucille screeching, "Dear Looooisss! Happy Buuuurthday tooo Yuuuuu!" Embarrassing, but fun.

When I went to her office for my private, Dr. Davis told me like she had the first day to make sure the door was closed behind me. She lit a cone of incense and asked me as she blew out the match, "What are you going to do to celebrate your birthday, Louis?"

"My mom will probably give me some presents after dinner. And she usually makes a cake."

"Good," Dr. Davis said. "But what are you going to do to celebrate yourself?"

I twisted a little in my chair and smiled. She didn't

really expect me to answer that, did she? She was looking at me like she did.

"Nothing, I guess."

"Well, you should. I always celebrate my own birthday. If you don't, why should anybody else?"

"I don't know." I shrugged. "What do you do?"

"Never mind what I do. Think about what you want to do for yourself. Doesn't have a thing to do with anybody else. You'll know it when you think of it."

She pulled a cake box from her side drawer and told me to open it. She'd bought two big pieces of chocolate cake with coconut icing. I wasn't crazy about coconut, but it didn't matter. How could she have known?

Instead of ginger ale, she'd brought apple cider in her thermos. When we were almost finished eating our cake, she realized she'd forgotten these napkins in her pocketbook that said Happy Birthday on them. She pulled them out and put them on the desk. "Oh well"—she laughed—"I'll keep them for us. And we can have more parties anytime we want to."

I said less that Friday than I'd probably said since the first day we'd had a private. I'd never cried in front of her before and I didn't want to start.

The week before Thanksgiving, Mom announced it was time to see if my back was healed. I begged her to let me take the bandages off myself, but she wouldn't hear it. "Put a towel over yourself if you're so embarassed."

She sat on the toilet seat and slowly pulled the adhesive away from my skin. I closed my eyes and tried to concentrate on what Dr. Davis had said about a gift for myself. I still hadn't figured out what I wanted yet. Mom sighed loudly when she saw the place where the fork had gone into me.

"I hope you never make me do anything this crazy again, Louis. I just pray to God."

"No ma'am," I said. "I won't." I was thinking that the only way to stop her was not to be there. Maybe that was my gift.

20

By December, Mom was pretty sure Ben had a girlfriend he was going to see on the weekends. I couldn't imagine anyone waiting all week to see Ben. Girlfriend or not, though, for the past two months, Friday morning was usually the last we saw of him until Monday after work.

I daydreamed now more than ever about leaving. I kept thinking about Mom sending me to New York the first time, the tag pinned to my jacket, her running alongside the train shouting for me to make sure I did everything she'd said. I remembered how glad I felt when it went too fast for her to keep up, and I was alone, moving away from her and Ben.

There were days I wanted to tell Dr. Davis how much I wanted to disappear, but I hadn't told her any of the really important stuff, so it wouldn't make sense to start with this. In our privates, she said she wasn't worried about how long it took for me to tell her things. "We have the time," she'd say in her Jamaican accent. "I'm not going anywhere."

She wasn't lying exactly, although that's what it felt like when two weeks before Christmas, Dr. Davis told me she was going home to Jamaica and wouldn't be back until after New Year's.

"Am I not allowed to have a holiday?" she asked me.

"Yes, ma'am."

"Well then, take off that sour face you're giving me. I want to wish you a Merry Christmas, Louis Bowman."

She gave me a present. It surprised me, like the cake she'd brought for my birthday. It meant she thought about me when we weren't at Burgess.

She said it was only for a couple of weeks, but I said a real good-bye to her for myself in case I never saw her again. When I got home, I opened her present. It was a small blue book with blank pages. There was a note inside.

Louis,
 Remember. It doesn't matter how much or how little you have to say.
 Never stop yourself from saying it.
       Your friend,
       Eleanor Davis

I sniffed the note. It smelled like hand cream.

When it was time to leave, I went outside and stood on the porch. Every day since I'd talked to Ray Anthony about Burgess, I thought he might come by maybe, to pick me up. The day Dr. Davis told me she was going away, I actually waited for him, as though I knew for sure he was coming. Then I decided to walk to Blackburn Avenue to the Sunoco station to find him.

The sun was sliding down behind the office buildings in the middle of town. The farther I walked in the opposite direction from the bus stop, the colder I got. When I got halfway down Blackburn Avenue, near the Sunoco station, I stopped. I didn't want Ray Anthony to see me. I wanted to watch him while I decided whether to go over and let him know I was there. I stood there, shivering, trying to figure out whether he was in the garage or inside the station. If he was on some kind of errand he hadn't taken the truck, because it was right there in the lot. There was an older man who I guessed was Ray Anthony's boss. He'd go in and out of the station and eventually I saw him go into the garage. When he came out again, he locked the door so I knew Ray Anthony couldn't be inside. I got closer as it got darker. I realized I must've been standing there almost an hour. Where was Ray Anthony?

Maybe he got off already, I thought. Or maybe he didn't have to work today. The older man got into a beat-up station wagon and started to back it out onto the street. When he passed me, I made sure I got a closer look at the man who'd hired Ray Anthony and saw him so much more than I did.

I stared at the empty Sunoco station and the truck Ray Anthony said he'd drive through Burgess if I needed him to. Maybe he'd lied. Maybe he didn't work at the station at all. Or maybe he'd been fired. Maybe Ray Anthony was the liar. liarsneakliar.

Wherever I thought I was going, I was going alone and no one was going to come driving through any buildings to give me a ride.

It didn't matter. I still wanted to see him. His red, fuzzy hair and pointy shoes. His chipped tooth and the space in between that I'd stopped trying to imagine filled in. I wanted to see Ray Anthony Robinson. Even if I never said it out loud, I wanted to begin saying good-bye.

21

Ben died the week before Christmas in his green Pontiac. The radio was playing "Jimmy Mack" instead of "Don't Sit Under the Apple Tree." He had a heart attack while I was punching him, shouting I hated him, I wanted him to die. I never expected that he really would.

After the ambulance took the body away, Mom and Lorelle and me went back to the apartment. Mom stopped in the kitchen, and stared into the sink. She picked up a dishrag and started scrubbing down the refrigerator door like she could see dirt on it that no one else could.

"Mom? Mom, you've still got your coat on."

She kept washing around the handle, using her fingernail to scrape a patch of dried jelly. Suddenly she stopped and went to the hall closet. She took off the grizzly, threw it onto the closet floor and kicked it into a corner. Then she went back to the refrigerator, scrubbing in circles the same places she'd just left shining.

That night, she carried Lorelle into my room in the dark, whispering to her, "We're going to sleep with Louis, just for tonight." But she didn't sleep. She sat up and smoked cigarettes till she finished the pack. Then, she smoothed the blanket over her thighs for hours with a juice glass of scotch as if she was ironing a deeply wrinkled skirt.

•   •   •

She came back from shopping for Ben's casket the next morning and told me, "I did the best I could. It's not exactly top of the line, but it's not like I had top-of-the-line money to work with either."

She explained she'd been shown a range in price and style she'd never expected. Oates, the undertaker, had taken her through a house with two floors of coffins on display in the black middle-class section of town.

"It's where the man lives!" she whispered, sinking into the couch like we were watching a late-night horror movie together, "and the only room I saw that didn't have a coffin in it was the front office."

She tucked her legs under her the same way she told me and Lorelle not to when we sat on the couch. "Well, all I can say is we won't have to be embarrassed or feel guilty either. Jesus only knows what would have happened if it had been me. The man would have put me in a cardboard box and never looked back." I knew she wasn't talking about Oates, the undertaker.

I didn't see what Mom had to choose from, but the deep brown box we sat in front of together at Oates Funeral Parlor looked respectable enough to me. Mom didn't remember Oates showing her the room where he'd put Ben, in front of a fake fireplace with wallpaper that was supposed to look like brick. In between people coming over to her and paying their respects, she leaned down to me and said, "It just shows you how crazy I must've been. He had to have said this was where the viewing would be. All I can remember are the rooms with those damn empty coffins and the big yellow price stickers on them like it was Sears."

People kept coming into the room where we were and

realizing they had the wrong wake. The whole time Mom looked like she was either studying for a test or taking one, I couldn't make up my mind which.

She must have been freezing at the funeral. Instead of the grizzly, she wore a thin, navy blue spring coat over her new gray suit. The grizzly was the warmest coat she had, but I could tell she wouldn't have worn that if it was the *only* coat she had. After the funeral, she said she thought sure she'd caught pneumonia, but she didn't talk about why she hadn't pulled the grizzly out from the bottom of the closet.

I didn't see the veil until we were ready to leave for the church. It looked like the ones Jackie Kennedy and Coretta King wore, except when I looked at Mom in hers, it was like looking at her through a screen door. If she never wore that veil again, I'd remember how it fell like a black cloud onto her shoulders. And her eyes, lined and shadowed under it, because she wanted to make sure people could see them through the cloud. Miss Odessa came to the apartment before we left for the church and said about a million times, "Girl, you don't have nothin' but some class. Leave it to you to look like the president's wife."

The church was almost full, but there were mostly regular members who came out of respect more than anything else. Ben didn't have any other family and I'd heard Mom tell Grandaddy on the phone it wasn't necessary to make the trip. She'd hired a baby-sitter for Lorelle, so it was just Mom and me sitting in the front row staring at Ben's coffin. Mom was half hidden to everyone else. I was the only one close enough to see her face under the veil. I wanted my own veil, one that was long enough to cover my whole body.

When the service was over, we got up and followed six men rolling Ben's coffin on a metal carrier to the door of the church. As we got into the funeral parlor limousine, I wanted to ask Mom if I had to get out again at the cemetery or if I could wait in it until she was through and then ride home. The wooden box was spinning around and around in my mind, planting itself deeper in my memory. I didn't want to add to what I'd already never forget.

But I stood beside her at the gravesite anyway. I stared at her through the veil and she murmured, "It's alright. It is." I wasn't sure she was talking to me, but I listened anyway and said it back to her in case she needed to hear someone else say it.

Miss Odessa tried to come back to the apartment with us to cook dinner, but Mom made it clear she didn't need her to do anything for us. She actually stood at the door and didn't let her come in, saying, "If we need anything, I'll call you. I promise."

Mom sat at the kitchen table. Lines I'd never seen before moved from her forehead to around her mouth. I felt helpless to do anything except give her some privacy. I started upstairs, but she called out to me, "Don't lock yourself in that room, Louis. I have to talk to you."

She sat across from me at the kitchen table with Lorelle half asleep in her lap. "I'm sending you to your grandaddy's till it's time for you to go back to school. I have enough on my mind without having to worry about your craziness. I don't want any more trouble."

Now? I thought. Why? What about Christmas? Am I supposed to sit in New York on my grandfather's couch staring out the window on Christmas while he sits in his room fixing old radios?

I went upstairs to the bathroom. Locked the door. Walked over to the bathtub in darkness and got in, sitting with my back to the faucet. Closed my eyes. *Don't tell anybody, Louis. Promise you won't tell anybody. On top of everything else, you're a liar. A sneak and a liar. Don't tell anybody. Promise you won't tell.*

"Louis!" She was running beside the train. "Louis!" She was at the foot of the stairs calling me.

Now it was clear to me. This was the time. I wasn't coming back from New York. Mom said herself how black kids disappeared off the face of the earth and nobody seemed to give a damn. There was one kid from the Stratfield Projects people still talked about. To hear Miss Odessa tell it, his own parents were sure everybody concerned was better off.

"Louis!"

Don't tell anybody. Promise you won't tell. I wished I'd known in enough time to tell Dr. Davis. Merry Christmas, Dr. Davis, I'm going away. At least I'd wished her a Merry Christmas. She'd know one day that Merry Christmas really meant good-bye.

I opened the bathroom door. Mom was already halfway up the stairs.

"What were you doing in there? Why didn't you have the light on?"

"Nothing. I wasn't doing anything."

"I told you. No craziness. Come downstairs and sit with me."

I started downstairs and stopped. I'd forgotten something.

"I'll be down in a minute." I ran back up to the bathroom. Turned on the light. Grabbed my towel and wiped my footprints from the inside of the tub. Black kids disappear all the time. *Don't tell anybody. Promise you won't tell.*

"Louis. This is the last time I'm going to ask you. What are you doing up there in the damn bathroom?"

"Nothing. I'm not doing anything."

I turned off the light and started downstairs again.

"I'm coming, Mom," I called to her. "Here I come."

22

She said it was raining bullets, but it was really only drizzling. It was the kind of rain you can barely see from your window but once you're in it, wraps itself around you until all you feel is wet. Mom slammed out into it with Lorelle to buy lunch meat for me to take to New York. She was annoyed because I said I couldn't go. I told her I wasn't packed yet, but I really needed the time alone to sneak more stuff into my suitcase. It didn't take me that long, because when I thought about it, it didn't make sense to make it too heavy. It was better not to take some things than to have to throw them away later on because I couldn't carry them.

It was the first time I'd been alone in the apartment since Ben's death. The whole time I was packing, I kept imagining he was in the next room.

Mom still hadn't slept in their bedroom alone at all. Lorelle would ask if she could sleep in Mom's room and Mom was still bringing her into mine. I thought if Mom was that scared she might change her mind about sending me to New York, but I guess she figured after I was gone there'd be more room in my bed for the two of them.

I took my suitcase downstairs and put it next to the door. Being downstairs didn't make me stop thinking about Ben being upstairs so I put on my jacket and went outside. I went over to the courtyard. With my face turned up into the rain, I counted eighteen rows of windows. There were twenty across. I stood in the middle of the courtyard and said to them, "You keep your eye on the center ring. Watch Louis Bowman disappear."

I walked back to the apartment, got a dish towel from the kitchen and dried my face with it. I smiled, thinking how Mom would have strangled me if she'd caught me. Then I folded it neatly and hung it back over the sink.

Sandwiching myself between the front door and the screen door, I waited for them. When they came around the corner, before Mom could say anything, I yelled out to her, "Just wanted to make sure I was ready when you got here!" I grabbed my coat and pulled the door closed behind me, locking Ben in.

At the bus stop, Lorelle asked me if she could go to Grandaddy's too, then she asked Mom. Mom didn't answer. She looked relieved that I was leaving. Having me around was probably like looking at the grizzly. A reminder, but one she couldn't easily kick into the corner of the closet.

When the bus came, I kissed Lorelle and as I got closer to Mom, I saw how streaked her makeup was. Different shades of brown running from her forehead to her chin. Her face is always wet, I thought. She's either sweating or crying or there's makeup raining down her cheeks. I wanted to dry her face like I'd dried my own, to tell her, "It'll be alright now. I'm leaving. No more sweating, no more crying. No more."

She didn't run alongside the bus yelling any instructions. I made a picture for myself of her standing there with Lorelle holding on to her under a black umbrella that used to be Ben's. I took my picture fast. I didn't look back again until I was pretty sure she'd started walking in the other direction.

But she never moved. Ben's umbrella was hanging at her side open, catching rain. I could still look into her eyes.

Go home, Mom, I whispered. It's alright, now. He's gone and so am I. You can go home.

23

He had to have been at the station, or at least on the platform, but I didn't see him. Not until I was already on the train with my suitcase on the seat next to me, hoping no one would sit down. Maybe I didn't see him because I was thinking about my suitcase being too heavy for me to carry around for very long. Or because I was thinking maybe I shouldn't get off in Harlem at all, but stay on until Grand Central Station where there were more people and it would be easier to disappear in the crowd.

"You doin' some travelin', huh?"

It was Ray Anthony Robinson. As many times as I'd thought about him, I'd never actually seen him anywhere but the projects. It was strange to see him outside them.

"I'm going to New York," I said. I couldn't tell him I wasn't coming back.

"Who you know in New York? You goin' for Christmas?"

Ray Anthony pulled my suitcase off the seat and lifted it to the overhead rack. He twirled the toothpick between his lips with his tongue and made this laughing sound in his throat. "Who's gonna carry this shit for you once you get there?"

He sank into the seat next to me and threw his feet up on the one across from us as if it was his living room couch. He had on maroon shoes, patent leather with

155

pointy toes. His jacket was leather too, short and curved in at the waist like a matador's. It smelled like vanilla extract, maybe because it was wet.

"My grandfather lives there." It was all I could get out. I sat there looking at him sideways, trying to think of what else to say. I wanted to tell him something that sounded important, something he'd remember if he never saw me again. While I concentrated on that, Ray Anthony folded his hands across his stomach, tipped his hat down over his eyes. I watched as he appeared to nod off to sleep. His stomach moved higher then lower, the corner of his mouth shining each time his tongue brushed over it. When the conductor whined, "One Hundred and Twenty-fifth Street next stop," I still hadn't made any decision about what I wanted to tell Ray Anthony or whether I should get off in Harlem or not.

I leaned closer to him and took a deep breath. I could still smell his jacket. It hadn't dried. "I might be staying here. I might not be going back."

He lifted his hat, slid it farther back on his head and turned to me slowly. I thought he might be mad because I woke him up. He looked at me so hard I moved back in my seat.

"How come?"

I didn't know how to answer, so I shrugged.

"Your mom's sendin' you away?"

I looked out the window. We were already in Harlem. I decided at that moment to get off. My grandfather would be waiting on the platform. I looked back at Ray Anthony. I wanted to wear his maroon patent leather shoes and his leather coat. What it would be like to step off the train as somebody so different from Louis Bowman?

"You got a piece o' paper?" he asked me. He stood up

and shook the wrinkles out of his purple pants, except there weren't any.

"In my suitcase." I reached for it, but he beat me to it. I couldn't have gotten it down by myself anyway. Inside, on top of everything else was the blue book with blank pages Dr. Davis had given me. I'd clipped a pen to the first page. I handed my book to him.

"Whatcha got in here?" He laughed and I stared at his chipped front tooth. I watched him leaf through the empty blue book and thought, if it was anybody else. Anybody.

"Nothing's in it," I told him. "I just got it."

Ray Anthony unclipped the pen and wrote, covering the whole first page. The sleeve of his jacket was so tight it looked like he had leather muscles. He held the book open and pointed to what he'd scrawled. "This is my mom's apartment, you know, where I stay."

I pushed the book into the suitcase quickly and kept my hand there so he wouldn't see it shaking.

The conductor called again, "One Hundred and Twenty-fifth Street." People around us were starting to get up and move down the aisles.

I nodded toward the window. "That's my grandfather."

Ray Anthony blocked me from getting to the aisle. He stood with his legs spread apart like he had that day behind the bushes, only this time he had both hands on his hips, holding his jacket open.

"Y'alright?"

"Yeah. I gotta get off."

He laughed. "Shoot, I gotta get off, too. Friday night. One Twenty-fifth Street and Christmastime, too. Whatchu think?"

What I thought was that this was the time most people

157

were going *home* for Christmas. I looked at the dent in his chin. Cleft. It was called a cleft chin. It was deep enough to stick my finger in. I looked down toward his shoes. That was the safest place. There was a key chain with a red rabbit's foot and a nail clipper lying on the seat.

"You dropped your rabbit's foot," I told him.

He picked it up and tried to slide it back into his pants.

"Can't have no luck without my foot." His pants were too snug for him to get it very far down into his pocket. It looked like he might lose it soon. I hoped he didn't believe in it too much.

Stepping back, Ray Anthony let me pass. I started down the aisle, but I was still picturing the cleft. I could see my finger pressed firmly into the middle of his chin.

When I stepped onto the platform, I studied my grandfather's face, trying to figure out if I should introduce him. I thought I heard Ray Anthony behind me, asking again, "Y'alright?"

"Yeah. I am. I'm alright."

I turned around ready to tell him, "This is my grandfather," but he was already going down the stairs toward 125th Street.

On the bus, I thought about whether I'd lied to him when I'd told him I was alright. Dr. Davis used to tell me she didn't trust it whenever I said it. She said she considered it a way of saying something was wrong, but I didn't want to talk about it. I disagree, though. For me, it's like the time I went to the dentist and Ellease, Dr. Horne's receptionist, told me I had to wait before he could see me. Inside his office, I could hear Dr. Horne calling, "Are you alright, Gladys? Are you alright?"

Ellease kept getting up from her desk and peeking into the office. When she came out, she'd look at me, slowly shake her head no, and roll her eyes. The fourth time she did it, I thought it would be okay to ask her, "What's the matter?"

Ellease whispered, "It's Mrs. Bentley. Dr. Horne gave her gas to pull her teeth and she passed right out. He thinks he might've killed her." Ellease looked at me, then down into her lap. I could tell she was stifling a laugh.

The office door opened and Dr. Horne came out with his arm around this elderly, mud-colored woman who wasn't any taller than I was, but probably weighed less. There was something familiar about her. I wondered for the first time what Mom would look like when she got old. The woman was creeping across the floor like the soles of her shoes had glue on them. I could see her trembling as she came toward me. Her grayed knot of a head, her whole body, trembling. She held her hands out in front of her like she was blind, feeling her way.

"Tell me now, Gladys. How do you feel now?" Dr. Horne asked her. "Can you feel the floor?"

The old woman stopped. She took a breath and at first, nothing. Then she said straight out into the room, "Yes. I can feel the floor, now. I can feel the floor." She smiled. "I'm alright."

That was what I'd wanted to tell Ray Anthony. That I thought I could feel my feet hitting the ground. I could feel the floor.

My grandfather and I got off the bus at 162nd Street and I asked myself, to make sure. Can you feel the floor, Louis? Can you feel the floor? Yes. Sure, I can. I can feel the floor.

Sitting on my grandfather's couch looking out onto the street, I thought more about Ray Anthony than I did about running away and wondered what he was going to do in New York. He was probably going to somebody's Christmas party in his purple pants and leather coat. There'd be people there his own age, not like the young kids who were at Delilah Buggman's party.

When he'd asked me, "You ain't got no number where you're goin'?" I wished I'd asked him back, "Where are *you* going?" Was he going to be at some guy's house, or a girl's? When I thought about it being a girl, I tried to picture her, but it made me nervous or sad or something. It was a friend's house, I decided, or maybe a relative's, and I tried to imagine what Ray Anthony slept in when he wasn't sleeping on trains. I slept in pajamas. Some guys, I knew, slept in their underwear or said they did, but Mom said that was a real nasty habit, so I didn't have a choice. I couldn't imagine Ray Anthony in pajamas, though. When I sat there and blocked out 162nd Street, closing my eyes to picture Ray Anthony sleeping, it wasn't in a bed. It was on a couch like the one I was sitting on and he was wearing his purple pants and that was all. I couldn't see his face. I could see only his bare feet hanging off the end of the couch and his back, long and wide and brown. His round butt jutted off the side of the couch. And when I couldn't stop staring at that, there was his fuzzy red hair, nappy and flat on his head. I tried to make him turn toward me, but he wouldn't. I thought, if only he'd turn this way, I could get up closer. I could see his lips shine when he runs his tongue over them. But his back kept me where I was, watching from farther away. I couldn't stop looking at this smooth, brown wall, praying for it to move. But I couldn't get any closer to it, either. I fell asleep picturing Ray Anthony.

Grandaddy woke me up and told me to pull down the

shade and put the sheet on the couch. "Why're you sitting in here, sleeping in your clothes?"

"Sorry," I told him. I wasn't, though. I spread the sheet over the couch, turned out the light and got undressed. I stood there for a moment in my underwear before I put on my pajamas. Held my breath and posed like the oily men on the covers of the muscle magazines. I should sleep like this, I thought. Like other guys. There's nobody here to stop me. But that would make me the sneak Mom already thinks I am. She'd be right, after all. Liarsneakliar. I pulled the shade, got into my pajamas and slowly, carefully laid down on the couch.

He was still there. He had his wall of a back to me, but he was still there.

24

People are always trying to get somewhere in Harlem, at all hours of the day and night, even in snowstorms. In Stratfield, people stay inside during bad weather. Even when it isn't bad, after the early morning when there are people everywhere, they all disappear until two-thirty when the kids get out of school. Occasionally, from the window at school I'd see one or two cars or a couple of guys driving delivery trucks. But walking the streets in the middle of the day? You might see a mother pushing a stroller once in a while, or a mangy dog wandering down the street like he owns it, peeing on every other tree and stopping to scratch. Other than that, Stratfield keeps itself inside, waiting for some kind of signal. In Harlem, everybody's moving all the time. Even the dogs in Harlem look they've got someplace to go, like they have to pee fast and move on.

I woke up Saturday, knowing I had to make a decision about running away. It seemed like a pretty stupid idea by then, especially since we were in the middle of a snowstorm, but I wasn't sure. Grandaddy was already up, drinking coffee in a white dress shirt and black, sharply creased wool trousers, as though he had a business appointment to keep. It was the way he always dressed, but as far as I could tell, he hardly ever went anywhere.

"I made grits," he said. "I left a fire under 'em so they wouldn't get cold."

I didn't much care for grits. When I went to the pot and saw how hard and dry they looked from sitting so long, I put a couple of tablespoons on my plate with a chunk of butter in the middle and mashed and stirred, hoping Grandaddy would finish his coffee soon and leave the kitchen. When he finally did, I sat there mashing and stirring some more trying to make my decision.

Grandaddy was in the middle of one of his radio projects. He had two of them taken apart and spread out on a sheet from the head to the foot of his bed. He sat on the side, chewing on an unlit cigar, picking up tiny wires and tubes and wiping them down with a dirty washcloth. A third giant radio, the color of eggplant with chipped gold numbers painted across the front of it like a crooked smile, was on the bureau playing the all-news station. I didn't usually go into Grandaddy's room, I waited until he came out before I said anything to him. But it felt like he'd tried to be friendly, making the grits for me, and I was trying to be friendly back without really knowing how.

I asked him, "You fixing these?"

"Yeah." He spoke through his teeth so the cigar never moved. I stood in the corner at first, really concentrating on him wiping each wire and screw, then just staring at the metal jigsaw puzzle on his bed and daydreaming until I felt my left leg go numb. Finally, I had an idea.

"Grandaddy? Sir, would it be alright if I . . . well, if I maybe took a walk?"

He looked up at me for the first time in almost two hours.

"A walk?! What kinda walk? There's a damn storm out there!"

"Just to get a paper. We're supposed to read the papers every day for school." It was true. I just didn't do it, usually.

"I get a paper most always," Grandaddy told me. "I woulda gone out myself if I'd known you wanted one. You need money?"

"No, I got some."

I went to my suitcase and got my envelope of running-away money. It was filled with loose change I'd stolen from around the house for the past few weeks. I hadn't bothered to count it, I knew it wasn't going to be that much and I didn't want to be disappointed. But it was better than not having any money at all.

I stuffed the envelope into my pocket and put on my jacket and hat. When I got to the door, Grandaddy yelled out, "You got boots? You need boots out there."

"No," I answered him quietly. "I don't have any boots. I mean I have some, but I didn't bring them."

"Why the devil would Jeanette send you out without any boots? She had to know it was gonna snow sooner or later. They been talkin' about this storm for days now."

I stood at the door, thinking I should let myself out quietly, when he came down the hall toward me, carrying a pair of old-man rubbers.

"Here. Stuff some paper bags in 'em if you have to. There's a stack under the sink in the kitchen."

"Thanks. Thank you, Grandaddy. Thanks." The rubbers were ugly and a little big, but not by much. I wasn't going out wearing any paper bags if I could help it.

I ran downstairs and around the corner, laughing. Now I was one of the people someone might be watching from the window of one of the old gray tenement buildings hurrying to get somewhere in Harlem. At the other end of the block was a phone booth. I emptied all my change out onto the metal ledge, unzipped my jacket and pulled out my blue notebook. I slid in a dime and dialed the operator.

"Long distance, please. To Stratfield, Connecticut."

I didn't really think Ray Anthony would be at home. I was pretty sure he was still in New York waiting to go to another party tonight, Saturday night. Like he'd said to me, "Shoot. Whatchu think?" I only called his number in Stratfield to hear his phone ring because he told me I could. When the operator told me to, I dropped several more quarters in and waited. I almost dropped the phone when it stopped ringing and a woman's voice answered flatly, "Yes?" I'd never heard anyone answer the phone like that before. She sounded as if she'd already made up her mind she wasn't especially interested in talking to whoever was at the other end of the line.

I was trying to think quickly whether I should ask for Ray Anthony, on the chance that he was there.

"Yes?" the woman repeated. It had to be Mrs. Robinson. I should tell her, I thought, "It's Louis Bowman. I live across the courtyard. Is Ray Anthony at home, please?" But I didn't.

The voice said, "If you're the same one who keeps callin' for Ray Anthony, he's still not here and I don't know when he's comin' back. Now, please don't keep ringin' this phone!"

I held my breath and waited for her to hang up first. I wondered who else called him enough for her to say that? I never saw him with anybody. If we ever got to be friends, I'd wait awhile, then I'd ask him.

Walking back to my grandfather's, I repeated to myself the rhythm in Mrs. Robinson's voice when she said, "Now please don't keep ringin' this phone!" Upstairs in the apartment, I whispered it so Grandaddy wouldn't hear me. I sat by the window and tried different ways of saying it, sounding even more exasperated than she had. I put my hands on my hips and imitated how she probably knotted up her face when she realized whoever it was was calling Ray Anthony again.

"What're you doin'?"

I jumped. "Nothin'." My grandfather was standing in the doorway. I didn't know how much he'd seen. "I was just talking to myself."

"You get a paper?"

I'd completely forgotten about it.

"No. They were sold out already. The guy said they didn't get that many causa the storm." I thought of how my mother said I was the quickest liar she'd ever known.

Grandaddy stared at me like he still wanted to know what I thought I was doing sitting on his couch with my hands on my hips pretending to be some woman, but he went back into his room without asking me. After a couple of hours he came back out. I was still on the couch, going through a pile of his old *Ebony* magazines.

"You goin' around the corner tomorrow morning?"

"Yes sir." I hadn't thought about going to church at all. But it was another excuse to get out. Even if I couldn't sneak my things out with me, I'd be by myself again. My trip to the phone booth made me think there were all kinds of possibilities once I got out into the street alone.

"Yes, I'm going." I went back to the *Ebony* article I was reading about Eartha Kitt, "Down to Earth with Eartha." When I was sure Grandaddy was back in his room, I told the ghost of somebody at the other end of the couch, "Please don't keep ringin' this phone." Only this time I did it in my Eartha Kitt voice. It sounded like I was gargling.

25

Gingerbread women. Filing through the snow in their Christmas garden hats. Mink tails looped over gold net. Purple and green velvet bubbles. Red satin helmets with cascading silver stars. They weaved into Greater Faith Harlem Baptist Tabernacle in twos, one arm linked to another's, steadying each other on the snowy pavement. A little weary but content, they looked as though they'd been traveling in pairs for years. Finally, they were home, the Sunday before Christmas.

I trailed behind in Grandaddy's old-man rubbers, almost to the entrance. I'd planned on sitting in the back. After an hour with the Greater Faith ladies, singing, swaying, and clapping for the birth of Baby Jesus, I'd slip out without being noticed and take a walk through the neighborhood. But when I got right up to the door, it occurred to me that I should take advantage of all the time I had outside by myself. Maybe if I walked long enough, I might walk into Ray Anthony.

Not really knowing Harlem or where exactly I was going, I headed downtown, deciding on 100th Street as a stopping point. I'd see how I felt once I got there. It could also be kind of a rehearsal so if I did run away . . .

Run away. It was sounding more and more like one of those TV shows about little white boys who packed peanut butter sandwiches and took their dogs with them. They usually got picked up by two cops who, before they

167

saw the kid, were sitting in their car looking straight ahead, trancelike, at an empty street. When they questioned the boy, they'd wink at each other the whole time they were talking to him. They knew he couldn't have anything to run away from. So they'd drive him home to his mother and sure enough she'd open the door wearing a ruffled apron, high heels and button earrings. He'd be just in time for an extra helping of pot roast, once he ran upstairs and washed his hands. I hardly saw any cops in Harlem and when I did they weren't jumping out of their car to ask any kids if they were lost.

I'd gotten as far as 128th Street. No Ray Anthony. No one that even looked like him. I thought about turning around right then but I convinced myself I should keep walking, just in case he was only blocks away and I'd miss him if I gave up.

One hundred and twenty-fifth. I couldn't walk any faster. Grandaddy's rubbers kept sliding off and I'd have to stop and pull them back onto my heels. There was a woman on the other side of the street with her little girl, waiting to cross. I thought of Mom and Lorelle at the bus stop in the rain before I left, Mom looking like she was still in that front seat with Ben, in the middle of the fight. It hadn't been the biggest they'd had, but it was the worst because he'd died during it, so it definitely wasn't a win for her. She'd survived it, maybe, but I could see she wasn't considering that a big victory.

Maybe I should go back, I thought. Maybe with only the three of us left . . . I stood there on the corner of 125th Street and watched the woman and her little girl cross over to where I was. I turned and followed them back uptown.

If I'm lucky, I'll see him now.

I looked in windows on both sides of the street. If I saw somebody even out of the corner of my eye who looked like he might be Ray Anthony, I'd go back and wait for the guy to come to the window again to make sure.

He'll be just getting up and stretching, looking outside to see how much snow has fallen.

Once I started this game, I knew it would take me twice as long to get back to 161 Street.

When I did get back, I clomped up to Greater Faith thinking I'd sneak in for the rest of the service. There couldn't be that much left. It felt like I'd been walking for hours.

I knew before I got to the doors of the church that I was too late. With Greater Faith, you could hear the service from halfway down the block. Not only did I know service was over, I knew I couldn't tell my grandfather I'd ever gone at all. Wearing a plastic-covered cap and a long black coat with a wide belt, he was there with his back to me staring toward the empty church.

I almost ran backwards in the other direction when he turned sharply as though he'd heard me thinking. He stared like he was making sure it was me. He's probably strong enough to knock me down with one punch, I thought, and then maybe it'll be over. But when he got closer, his own face was too full of fear for me to be afraid for myself.

"Where were you?" he rasped.

"I didn't feel well. I was dizzy and I had a headache. I thought I was gonna faint. I had to leave to get some air."

I dared to look into his eyes and was ashamed at what I could see him thinking. liarsneakliar. He walked past me and I followed. We hadn't taken three steps when he turned back to me.

"You know this isn't the time for no mess, boy. Jeanette's

in a hard place. She's got responsibilities, she's got your younger sister. You should be there with her. You can't be actin' crazy or gettin' lost nowhere or startin' some damn foolishness crap. You should go back and do what you can. You hear me?"

"Yes sir." I said it quickly, like I didn't have to think about it, as if I knew exactly what he meant which of course I did. It was strange how he sounded like he knew everything I might be thinking now when he'd never seemed to know anything about me before. We walked toward the apartment in silence, climbed six flights and all I could hear was the sound of our footsteps and his sigh each time he got to a landing.

While he was locking us in, I hung up my jacket quickly and went to the front room, to the couch. I sat as still as possible, the closest I could get to being invisible.

"You come here, Louis."

So he waited, I thought. He waited until we got here to beat me. He was in the kitchen. I went to him telling myself nobody's beating lasted forever. Grandaddy had never hit me before. He hardly ever touched me at all.

"Yes sir?" I looked at him like I was used to looking at Mom, the same as I'd looked at Ben every Sunday before the boxing matches. I told him with my eyes, you don't have to do this, you know. It's not really necessary. You just think it is now. Later, you'll regret it.

Grandaddy was sitting next to the stove, still in his coat. His cap was in his hands, dripping snow onto the kitchen floor. When I stood in front of him, we were face to face, close enough to kiss. I could see my mother in his mouth and eyes. When he spoke I heard her voice in his, especially the way it had sounded years before when I was very young.

"It's not good now. But it's not good for anybody. Everybody's sittin' at the same end of the table."

"Yes, sir."

"You got to go back. She needs you to be there with her. You don't know she needs you?"

"Yes, sir, I know."

"Tomorrow. You all should be together for Christmas, you're a family. Jeanette's gotta be upset outta her mind to send you here right before Christmas. She's not thinking clear. That's what it is." He stood and I backed out of his way. The only other thing we said to each other was when I got on the train the next day to go home. I said, "Good-bye, Grandaddy. Merry Christmas." He said, "Remember."

I don't know if he called her before I got to Stratfield and if he did, how much he told her. But she was waiting at the station with Lorelle. Jumping in front of the conductor, she pulled me off the train and squeezed the breath out of me. She held my head down into her coat like it was a football she was going to make a run down the platform with to score a touchdown.

"Mom?" I called into her chest. Her wedding band was cutting my ear. It was no use. Mom never let you out of a hug until she was ready.

The next morning, Christmas Eve, I was on my knees scrubbing the bathroom floor when she came in behind me. I waited, thinking she was inspecting my work and would either leave in a minute, which meant the floor would pass or tell me to scrub harder, which was what usually happened. Instead, she stood over me slowly tugging on her fingers like she was pulling off a pair of gloves that were too small.

"I asked forgiveness while you were gone. I don't want to ever have anything to do with you getting hurt again. I want you *here*. Safe."

Why didn't she ask *my* forgiveness? I thought. Wasn't *I* the one she should ask? After she left, while I rinsed the tiles to make sure they weren't gritty from the cleanser, I figured what she'd told me was her way of apologizing. I'd rather she'd just come out and say she was sorry, but I knew what she'd said was as close as it was going to get.

While I was in New York, people from the church had brought Mom a Christmas tree and groceries. There were three presents under the tree, one for each of us with a card signed "Merry Christmas, from your friends at Stratfield Methodist." I knew Mom had more hidden away. If she'd put up the tree at all, it was because she had her own gifts for Lorelle and me like always. No matter who'd died, a present apiece from strangers wasn't her style.

The presents I'd bought had been under my bed for almost a month. The night before I went to New York when I thought I might not be coming back, I considered giving Mom hers and Lorelle's, but I was still too upset about her sending me away at Christmas. I pictured her finding my wrapped packages covered in dust and cobwebs maybe in April or July and wishing she had a prayer of thanking me in person.

I'd bought a bottle of her favorite perfume, Blue Gardenia, as part of a Bloomingdale's Blue Gardenia Christmas special. It came with a smaller bottle of Blue Gardenia lotion, two bars of Blue Gardenia soap and a blue antique soap dish with glass legs and the initials *BG* on them. I already knew Mom wouldn't like the soap dish because she didn't buy things with other people's initials or names on them. She said they looked as though they were either inherited or stolen.

I got a knitted hat and scarf for Lorelle and a Carl the Crocodile puppet like the one she watched every day on television. Carl the Crocodile was huge with bumpy greenish gray skin, big plastic teeth and eyes that rolled around in its head. Mom said not to bother with the puppet because it was too expensive to be so ugly and she didn't care if Lorelle liked it or not, she didn't want to have to look at it. What Mom didn't know was that I'd bought Carl before I told her about it and he was nonrefundable, so I'd gotten the hat and scarf set as a backup. There was also a bottle of Bay Rum aftershave that would have been for Ben.

Mom always gave me money and told me to make sure I got Ben a gift. I always told her not to worry. I wouldn't have given a present to her and Lorelle and not given one to him. Even though I knew he didn't buy any of the things with tags Scotch-taped to them that said "Love to Louis, from Mom and Daddy Ben."

Mom, Lorelle and I were all in my bed Christmas morning. Lorelle woke up at four and asked every half hour when we were going to get up to open presents. Mom got up around six, but she told Lorelle she couldn't go downstairs until at least seven and left me responsible for making sure she didn't. When the two of us went down an hour later, Mom was sitting on the couch with only the tree lights on.

"Is it alright to start Christmas now?" Lorelle asked her, wanting to make sure she hadn't done anything wrong.

"Sure it is." Mom said it so softly, I didn't want to look at her yet. "Sure it is."

26

I kept watch at the window to see if Ray Anthony was back from New York. Maybe he was staying straight through New Year's, it was only a couple of days away.

Thursday afternoon, I was in the kitchen setting the table for dinner when I heard Mom say, "You'd think somebody'd be too cold to strut around with their behind out like that in the middle of winter." I ran in to the living room and stood next to her at the window. Hallelujah! Amen! The very behind she was talking about was the same behind I'd been waiting for days to see.

"He thinks he's cute, parading around like that in those pimp pants," Mom said. "He thinks somebody wants to look at all that."

Well, if that's what he thought, he was right. Somebody did want to look at all that. Even so, as badly as I wanted to, at that moment it was impossible for me to run out of the apartment to see him any closer. The good news was that Ray Anthony was back home for sure. And so was I.

I watched from the living room window most of Thursday night and didn't see him again. After we were all in bed and I hoped Mom was asleep, I got up and sneaked downstairs to the phone. My plan was to let it ring long enough to see if he answered, just to let me know if he was there across the courtyard. But I'd hang up without telling him it was me calling. I got almost to the bottom of the stairs when Mom switched the hallway light on and yelled down, "What are you sneaking around for? All I need is for you to fall down a damn flight of stairs and break your neck. That's all I need."

I knew then she'd be listening to hear what I was doing, so I went to the kitchen, poured a glass of ice water and dumped it into the sink. So much for the phone call.

Friday morning, I decided I could save some time by not eating breakfast. Cleaned the bathroom, mopped the staircase, dusted the furniture and vacuumed, watching the courtyard the whole time. When Ray Anthony hadn't come out by noon, I thought about skipping lunch because I couldn't see the courtyard from the kitchen, but I was too hungry. I made a sandwich and ate it standing up at the sink, running back and forth into the living room to keep watch. The third time the door swung open to his apartment building, I threw my sandwich into the garbage, thinking it had to be him finally coming out.

Mom came to the kitchen door. "What the hell do you think you're doing, Louis?"

"Sorry, ma'am," I mumbled, immediately digging back into the aluminum pail for the brown bread and salami.

"Don't be a smart ass, Louis."

She came over and stared at me. "You've been acting like you're about to jump out of your skin all morning. Something wrong with you?" She searched my face for an answer.

"No, ma'am."

"You need to take all that energy outside. You think there's too much snow to take the bike out?"

"Probly. But I could go out anyway."

Now she really looked surprised. She knew how much I hated going outside just to be outside. It was like being a

BIL WRIGHT

magnet for whatever maniac in the projects who hadn't
knocked the crap out of me yet to get his chance. But
today, I was willing to risk it.

"I'll just sit on the stoop for a while and read."

"It's too cold for you to be sitting out there in one place
for long, but I'll let you find that out. Don't get yourself
sick, though. You can sit right upstairs in your room and
read."

I ran up, got dressed, and grabbed a book I'd taken out
of the library, *Ivanhoe*. It was a big, boring mistake, but it
was the only thing I'd brought home for Christmas vaca-
tion besides my algebra book. I got out of the apartment
as quickly as possible, before she changed her mind and
found something she'd rather have me do inside.

After about a half hour on the stoop, my butt hurt and
my fingers burned. I sat on *Ivanhoe* and blew into my
palms, but I was pretty sure I'd have to give up and go
back in soon. Mom came to the door and said through the
screen, "You haven't budged from this stoop. And you're
not reading either. I hope you have enough to sense to
come in before you get frostbite."

I turned back to her with a big, fake grin and felt my
bottom lip split. "I'm fine, Ma."

"Suit yourself." As she said it, I heard the door open
across the courtyard. I jumped up as though *Ivanhoe* had
suddenly caught fire. Mom frowned.

"Really, Ma. I'm fine," I told her twice as loudly as the
first time.

"I heard you." But she wasn't looking at me. She was
glaring at Ray Anthony Robinson, who was moving fast
and not even looking our way. Mom stepped back into
the room and shut the door in my face.

I knew she was probably watching from the window,

but I didn't care. I ran to catch up with him. He'd already made it to the parking lot. Running up to him from behind, I thought about what Mom had said and laughed. She was right. Ray Anthony did walk like he was proud of the perfectly round butt that seemed to be moving in the opposite direction he was. He didn't walk like she said I did sometimes. She told me, "That walk of yours is gonna get you killed." I knew I didn't walk like her imitations of me, but it wasn't anything like Ray Anthony's walk either. His walk didn't look especially to me like a man's or a woman's. It was more like watching a horse from behind. He had everything but the tail.

"Ray Anthony!"

He turned to look at me without stopping. Today it was the toothpick. If it wasn't a cigarette, it was a toothpick. Once I'd seen him with a toothpick, a cigarette *and* chewing gum.

I was right beside him, out of breath. Not because I couldn't keep up with him, but because I always got a little out of breath when I saw him. He walked fast, and his legs were longer, but I could definitely keep up. I was used to walking fast. Like Mom said, I'd grown up running, it was one of the things I did best.

"You're back." I looked for the cleft, but the collar of his jacket was pulled up and I couldn't see his chin at all.

"Uh-huh."

"I thought maybe you were still in New York. At your relatives'." He didn't say anything. Our feet crunching across the snow in the parking lot made us sound like we knew where we were going, like we had a purpose, the same purpose.

"I ain't got no people in New York."

I didn't know if I should keep walking and not try to

talk or find some topic of conversation he might be interested in.

"So you back too, huh?"

Thank God. A sign.

"Yeah, I been back for a few days. I was thinking about calling you, but I didn't know . . . you never said how long you'd be away."

He smiled, straight ahead. "That's why people call. Ta see."

"You're right. I should've called to see."

"Don't matter. My moms said I should stop givin' out her number cause it drives her crazy answerin' it all the time and it's always for me."

I wanted to tell him she certainly wasn't hiding from the caller how annoyed she was, but I thought better of it. "Oh," I responded, as if what he was saying hadn't ever occurred to me.

We'd made it out of the projects and down the street. I wished I'd left *Ivanhoe* on the stoop because now it felt like I was stuck with it and I needed to be free to go wherever Ray Anthony was going. Having *Ivanhoe* with me made me feel like I was still connected to the stoop, as though it had the power to propel me back there without warning. Sure, it was superstitious, but I made up stuff like that all the time.

The next thing I asked him I knew could ruin everything, but I took a chance.

"Can I walk wherever you're walking?" I got a glimpse of his chin. He hadn't shaved and the cleft was almost covered by beard. I wanted to tell him he should shave regularly so that his cleft didn't get covered up.

He snorted, making me think how wrong it had been to ask him. What was it that made him so friendly one minute and act as though he'd never seen me before, the next? Had he completely forgotten he'd said he'd drive through a building if I asked him to? Well, whatever it was and as aggravating as it was, I wouldn't press it, as Dr. Davis would say. And I wouldn't let it stop me. I just slowed down. Now he had a choice. He could either slow down with me or speed up and leave me behind. Or he could answer my question.

He didn't speed up, but he didn't answer either. Not at first. It wasn't until he got so far I almost couldn't hear him that he turned his head and said over his shoulder, "Do what you want."

As it turned out, he wasn't going far. Two streets away, he stopped on the corner at Big Lou's Cigarettes and Candy. It was the store everybody in the projects went to even though they all complained about how high Big Lou's prices were. Mom didn't shop there herself, but she sent me every morning before school to buy her Salems and a *Daily News*. I almost never went later in the day and I was surprised to see kids actually hanging out in front of it. I didn't know any of them. There were two girls and two boys. Actually, they were too old looking to be called kids. They were sixteen or seventeen, maybe eighteen even, definitely too old to be standing around shivering in the cold outside a candy store like they were waiting for someone to come by and take them home. The only one who looked like she had any purpose in being there was one of the girls. She seemed to be concentrating hard, writing in the snow on the hood of the car with a stick. She frowned as though she was struggling with an important message.

I figured they were probably from the other projects, Creighton Heights. It was farther over on the south side and had a reputation for being rougher than where we lived. Mom said to Ben once during an argument, "If it were up to you, we'd be over in Creighton Heights dodging bullets."

It didn't occur to me that Ray Anthony might know these people. When he got closer, one of the guys, a wide, lightskinned giant with a tiny head, yelled out, "Here come the man! Ray Anthony! Ray-Ray, whatcha say?!"

From where I was behind him, I could tell that Ray Anthony's walk changed. It didn't have as much music in it as before. He seemed to pull his butt in and spread his legs out more as if his back had suddenly gone stiff.

"That's a baaad jacket, my man! You pick that up in the city?"

Maybe Ray Anthony never answered anybody right away. He stopped, took the toothpick out of his mouth. He tapped the snow from his toes on the curb, as though it made sense to wear patent leather shoes in the snow and think that tapping could do much to protect them.

"Naw," he said. "I been had this."

I could hardly hear him from where I was standing. His voice was lower, huskier than I'd heard it before. I stood to the side of the street, behind a parked car at the other end of the block, trying to hide while I watched him, this new Ray Anthony.

"We waitin' on you, man. We got our buggy right here, we ready to ride!" The giant with the tiny head pointed to the car with the girl writing on the hood. Even under the snow the car looked tired, beat up, a dull black except for one shiny blue door on the driver's side. The blue door didn't look real, as if it wasn't actually attached to the rest of the car. It looked as if it might fall off at any minute.

"Where you wanna go, Ray-Ray? You wanna drive?" the girl who wasn't writing asked him.

Ray Anthony shrugged and told them, "Naw, I ain't drivin'. I don't feel like drivin'."

A woman came out of Big Lou's with a full bag of groceries in each arm. As she passed the kids in front of the store, she called out, "Rita, honey, I think your mama's lookin' for you."

The girl with the stick turned suddenly from the hood of the car and shouted, "I look like somebody's Rita-honey to you?" The girl had black, bowling ball eyes that looked even bigger because she'd penciled thick lines on her upper and lower lids and drawn them out at the sides.

The woman stared at her for a moment, surprised. She walked quickly between the cars and across the street shaking her head from side to side, mumbling something I couldn't hear.

They all laughed. I couldn't see whether Ray Anthony was laughing or not because he still had his back to me. The giant said, "Crita, you crazy."

"She's so stupid!" The girl was still shouting. "She don't know the difference between Crita and Rita, she need to keep her mouth shut. How she gonna be all in my business tellin' me my mama's lookin' for me an' she don't know my mama's Rita and I'm Crita?"

Whatever her name was, she was loud. She was shorter than any of them, but she looked like the oldest.

"Babyback, why don't you drive if Ray Anthony don't wanna? It's your car. Shoot, we waited all this time for him and now what are we supposed to do? Not go nowhere just cause he don't wanna drive?" As she said it, she stared up at Ray Anthony, daring him to argue with her. "I'm ready to go somewhere whether he go or not!"

Ray Anthony hunched up his shoulders. I wished I could get closer to see his face. Why would he let her talk to him this way? If he didn't want to be with them, he could go somewhere with me. I had to wait to see if maybe there was a chance.

"You oughtsta let me drive some damn time, Babyback. I don't know why you always axin' him anyway." It was the other guy, as tall as the giant, but darkskinned and as skinny as Babyback was wide.

"Nah huh! I ain't goin' nowhere with you drivin', Bones. Y'all talkin' about *I'm* crazy. Now *he* the one that's crazy, for *real* crazy! I ain't gettin' in the car if Bones be drivin'." Crita wrapped her open nylon jacket around her with the zipper hanging loose from one side. She pulled her green hairband farther down on her forehead so that her hair, no longer than the band was wide, stuck straight out away from her head like a halo of nails.

"Aw, Crita!" Bones pouted. "Ain't nobody wanna drive you no place no how."

I watched Ray Anthony's back for some sign of what he was going to do.

"If Ray Anthony don't wanna drive, then I'll drive," Babyback said. His side of the car sank to the curb when he got in and he looked upset when the door scraped loudly against the sidewalk as he pulled it shut. He rolled the window down and yelled, "What y'all waitin' for? Geraldine, you come on in front with me."

Geraldine giggled and went over to the other side and got in.

"Ray Anthony, you come on an' get in the back with Crita."

I held my breath. He turned around, yes he did turn around and look at me for just a moment before he went out into the street and got in Babyback's car. I tried to see if he was sending me a message that maybe he didn't want to go, or even if he did, he'd see me later. But if there was a message, I couldn't figure it out.

Crazy Crita jumped in behind him and slid over as close as she could, squeezing him into a corner behind Babyback in the driver's seat. Bones, left standing in the street, glared after Crita. He lit a cigarette and slouched around to the other side of the car.

Babyback said, "Oh, you comin' too, Bones? I didn't think you was comin'."

But by the time time Babyback finished, Bones had already climbed in and slammed the door. He was in the backseat on one side, Ray Anthony was on the other. I stepped out from where I'd been hiding behind the car. As the five of them pulled off, I could see the outline of Crazy Crita's halo of nails.

<u>27</u>

—Hello. Ray Anthony?

—You speakin' to 'im.

—This is Louis. Across the courtyard.

—Yeah, I know.

—You did? How'd you know?

—I could tell from the voice. I don't know nobody else talks like you do.

—Oh.

—So. What can I do for ya?

—Well, I wanted to call to wish you a Happy New Year. I was thinking I should do it now because you might be going to New York or something and I wouldn't get a chance.

—I ain't goin' to New York for New Year's.

—You're not?

—Naw, I ain't got no goin' to New York money.

—So you'll probably just go to some party or something around here, in Stratfield, huh?

—Somethin'. I don't know what it's gonna be yet.

— Maybe you'll . . . maybe you'll go to a party with those kids from Creighton Heights . . . uh . . . Babyback . . . and . . . uh . . . Crita.

—Maybe so. I tol' ya, I don't know yet.

—Oh . . . Ray Anthony?

—Yeah?

—Those kids. Are you really close friends with them?

—Whatchu mean, "close friends"?

—You know. *Close friends.* I didn't even know you knew them.

—Whatchu mean, you didn't know, you don't hardly know *me*. We hang out, that's what I do with them. You was lookin' at what I do with them.

— I think that Crita girl . . . likes you.

—Crita? She don't know what she like an' what she don't like from one minute to the next.

—I think she knows she likes *you*. I could tell.

—Yeah well, I ain't thinkin' nothin' bout Crita.

—What about that Bones?

—What about Bones? You gonna tell me he like me too?

—No. What I was gonna say was how come Crita said he was the one who was really crazy? Is he?

— You got to ask Crita. She the one who said it.

—Oh come on, Ray Anthony, you're friends with them. You probly know what she meant. Is he really crazy?

— You keep on comin' around him, see what you think. You want me to introduce y'all so you can ask him right out?

— No.

—Well then, why you gonna ask me all kinda questions then? Huh?

— I'm sorry, I guess, I mean, I thought . . . I just wanted to ask you about them cause I thought they were your good friends, that's all. I thought you'd wanna talk about them.

—I got to go.

—You mean get off the phone or . . . are you really going someplace?

— I mean both. I got to go.

—Well, me too. But I'll probly be looking out the win-

185

dow when you leave your house. If you look across, you'll probly be able to see me.

—Uh-huh.

—But if you forget, if you don't see me, I'll be around tomorrow too. I'm not going anywhere for New Year's either.

—Uh-huh.

—So I'll see you.

—Yeah.

I stood at the living room window and waited. Mom was upstairs, but I didn't care this time if she'd heard me or not. Three or four minutes later, Ray Anthony ran out of his apartment building and started across the court-yard. At the sight of him, my whole body was ready to wave, to say yes, that was me you were talking to, that was me and here I am now. Louis.

He didn't turn around until he was at the parking lot, but I knew that he would. When he did, I didn't wave at all. I smiled and he nodded. Then it was too dark for me to really see him, crossing the parking lot out onto the street. I wondered if he was going to Big Lou's. Would they be waiting for him, Crita and Geraldine, Babyback and Bones? How many other people waited for Ray Anthony like I did?

It was summertime in the dream. I was jumping the tracks. Feeling the heat through the soles of my sneakers. My bare legs burning in the sun. Skinny chicken legs, jumping the train tracks like a grasshopper in July.

There wasn't anything on either side of me that let me know exactly where I was, but New York City was up ahead, waiting for me in the distance. Behind me, the tracks curved like a line of Cs strung together. What looked like the old Stratfield station platform turned out to be Big Lou's Cigarettes and Candy. I walked toward the city staring back over my shoulder at it. Sweat rolled down my forehead and dropped from my eyelashes onto my cheeks. I yanked my T-shirt out of my shorts, wiped my face, my neck. When I looked again there they all were in front of the store, in their winter clothes. Babyback was holding on to the blue door of his car. The rest of the car wasn't there, just the door. No one seemed to notice the car was missing. They were all sneering at me. Crita called out, "You're lucky you got away. If you ever come back, you'll wish you hadn't."

When I turned away from them, the city wasn't in front of me anymore. There was just one building, the one my grandfather lived in, standing at the other end of the tracks. He was on the stoop, with his back to me, wearing his cap with the plastic cover and his long black coat. He even had on the rubbers he'd loaned me. I had the same sick feeling in my stomach as when I saw him outside Greater Faith Harlem Baptist. It didn't feel like I should be looking forward to New York any more than I should think about going back. I kept moving in his direction, though. He was my family and he hadn't hurt me before. The Creighton Heights Projects gang didn't have anything better to do.

When it looked like I was getting closer to my grandfather, I turned around toward Stratfield again. The four of them were moving up on me. I started to run. The tracks were so hot, it felt like my sneakers were melting under me. I've got to run faster. Faster. Someone was beside me, so close I could feel their breath on my neck. I could smell . . . Ed MacMillan. Ed MacMillan running beside me with his lying eyes and whining.

"Go away, you bastard. Go away!" I swung at him, aiming my fist at his mouth. My hand went right through his face, from one side to the other and out again. He wasn't hurt, he didn't seem to feel it at all. I ran faster. He couldn't keep up. The sound of his breath, his smell was gone.

I focused toward the city. My grandfather began to turn slowly on his stoop. Even before I saw his face, I could tell that it wasn't my grandfather anymore. It was another trap. Now, one of the goons from Creighton Heights was waiting for me on the other side too. But I couldn't stop running in his direction, my feet wouldn't do anything else. He turned. As he came around, his coat opened slowly and his cap flew off. There was a blaze of red, nappy hair.

The long black coat was gone. The only thing the man I ran toward had on was a pair of purple pants. Ray Anthony. I laughed. I wanted to see his face.

I ran faster. I could feel the Creighton Heights gang catching up. Faster still because the farther I got, the farther away Ray Anthony was. Slowly, he kept turning. I still couldn't see his face. Even when the rest of his body was turned toward me, he wasn't looking in my direction. I reached for his chest, his hair, his arms. Ray Anthony, I called to him. I couldn't hear my own voice, but I called anyway. Look. It's me. Louis. Reach for me, Ray Anthony. Reach. Please. Reach.

28

A kid in a dirty red coat with one button on it was wearing a silver paper hat with a rubber band under his chin. He kicked slush in the courtyard and told anybody who passed, "My mama's givin' a party tonight and she said *everybody's* comin'." He was the only sign of New Year's Eve in the projects.

Miss Odessa came by in the morning and asked Mom if she wanted to go to church with her later that night. Mom said it was too dangerous to have to walk home in the dark with all the drunks out and she'd just as soon stay home. After Miss Odessa left, Mom said the real reason she'd said no was because every time she'd gone to church with Miss Odessa, she'd talked about people all through the service.

"Number one, it gives me a damn headache and number two, it makes people think I've got a mouth just as vicious as hers. People curse that mouth of hers," Mom said, "and I don't want anybody cursing me on New Year's Eve. That's the worst kind of luck you can bring on yourself, somebody cursing you for the New Year."

"Well, I wish I was doing something tonight instead of sitting around here like I've done every New Year's since I was born."

Mom looked at me for a minute, with her eyebrows raised. "All of a sudden you're a party boy, huh? Well, you have a particular party you wanna go to, tonight?"

I sure do, I thought. If only I knew what Ray Anthony was going to do. Maybe, I thought, I should tell her something just to get me out of the house and I could find out if he'd let me go wherever he was going. But it was too fast for me to think it through and I wound up sucking my teeth and saying, "No. No party. I'll be here as usual."

"Well," she said, "I have a date tonight." I didn't believe her. Had she lost her mind? Who did she have a date with this soon after Ben's death and why didn't I know about him?

"Who with?" I asked her. I only hoped she wasn't going to name somebody terrible, somebody new to worry about.

"Well, he's kinda short, but I don't mind. Cause he's smart. Very smart."

Like Ben, I thought. At the beginning she'd been so impressed that Ben was smart.

"So he's smart, Mom. Big deal. There are a lot of smart guys around. Just not a lot in Stratfield. What's his name?"

"Maybe he's not as smart as I thought he was," she said, waving the dish towel in the air and doing a strange kind of waltz step in circles around the living room.

So she *had* lost her mind. Whoever this was was going to be trouble, I was sure of it.

"Boy, don't you know I have a date with you, Louis Bowman, and you have a date with me?"

I was embarrassed. I knew what a date was, even if I'd never had one. She was making fun not just of me, but of both of us, really.

"And I've asked Mr. Guy Lombardo and his orchestra to come right into our living room and play for us."

I sat on the couch, trying not to be rude, but also trying

to say enough, stop, I get the joke and it isn't funny, please stop.

"I want you to make a list of all the things we're gonna need to have ourselves a good time." She was already in the kitchen getting a pad and pen. When she came back, she caught me rolling my eyes at the living room ceiling.

"Well, aren't you a mess," she said, dropping the pad into my lap. "Turning up your nose at spending an evening with your mother. I'm not used to men turning up their noses at me, you know."

"What do you want me to write?" I wanted to get this part over with so she wouldn't have to talk about it anymore.

"Now you know I know how to give a party. Get a quart of ice cream and one of those little pound cakes. A bottle of ginger ale for you and then I want you to go to the liquor store and get me a little scotch."

"What's a little? A fifth? A pint? Don't you want champagne? It's New Year's."

"I'd want champagne if I could afford the kind I wanted to drink. Cheap champagne'll half kill you. After you've had the best, and I have, you don't want to depress yourself on New Year's Eve drinking the cheapest."

"I have to change my pants."

"To go to the grocery store? Why?"

I was already halfway to my room so I didn't have to answer. I wanted to put on a new pair of jeans she'd given me for Christmas. They were a size too small, but I liked the way they looked, because they were tight and made my legs look bigger and longer. I wanted to wear them to Big Lou's, just in case. I brought them into the bathroom with me along with a cigarette.

Every kid I knew either smoked or claimed they did but

I'd never seriously considered it before. Most people I watched didn't look like they particularly enjoyed it. What was the point? People in movies did it with a lot more style. Definitely, Ray Anthony was in the movie star category and actually most of the time so was Mom. Smoking looked good on Ray Anthony but so did toothpicks, chewing gum and patent leather shoes. Anyway, now I'd decided it was something we could have in common. The next time we talked and I ran out of things to say to him, I could offer him a cigarette and stall, thinking up a good topic while we lit up and took the first couple of puffs. I figured since I didn't have a car to let him drive like Babyback did, it was at least something I could offer him.

I practiced the whole thing with the cigarette I'd stolen from Mom. I turned in my tight jeans and looked up at Ray Anthony.

"You wanna cigarette? . . . Sure, I smoke. You didn't know cause you don't know me that well." I could see I'd made the right decision by his smile. I held out the pack and got the matches ready. I lit his cigarette and mine at the same time like the guy did for Bette Davis in *Now Voyager*. Ray Anthony'd probably never seen a Bette Davis movie in his life. He'd think it was something I came up with.

I only had it lit for a second, but a second was enough to set Mom's radar off. No sooner was I in my room than she came barreling right in without knocking.

"If you think you're gonna start the New Year off by smoking cigarettes in my house without my permission, you better think again, Louis."

I wished I'd brushed my teeth afterwards. Even though I'd only had a couple of puffs, I felt a little nauseous going to

Big Lou's. I held my mouth open while I was walking and stuck my tongue out in the air, but my mouth still tasted like I'd been chewing oregano.

I saw Babyback's blue car door down the block. He was standing in front of it alone outside the store, drinking a can of beer in a paper bag. He looked around him like he was either watching for cops or waiting for the rest of his gang to show up. Probably both. Did that mean Ray Anthony was on his way? I walked right up to Babyback but I didn't have the guts to ask him. I went into Big Lou's and couldn't get to the freezer for the pound cake or the ice cream because of the long line in front of the counter. While I waited, watching through the store window for Ray Anthony, I had an idea. I got out of line and went to the back of the store to the pay phone. I'd memorized the number by now. 326-8757. I was about to hang up when he answered on the sixth ring.

—Yeah?

—Ray Anthony?

—Who you think? You called my house, didn't you?

—It's me, Louis.

—Yeah, I know.

— I'm at Big Lou's. My mother sent me. And Baby-back's outside. He's alone. I passed him on the way in. I could be wrong, but it looked like he was waiting for you. I just wanted to know if you were coming.

So alright, he didn't like to be asked what he was doing or where he was going. If he was going to get mad, he could go ahead and get mad. Today I felt like taking the chance.

— I was thinkin' bout comin' over there in a while. Why? You hangin' with us now?

Maybe it was his sense of humor and I just didn't get it.

Maybe when I was around him long enough, it wouldn't bother me at all.

—No, I'm here at the store like I told you. But there's a line so I might be here a while. Maybe I'll see you. If you come soon.

—Yeah, well, don't wait for me or nothin.' I ain't even dressed yet.

— No, I won't wait. But I might still be here. I might, that's all.

I hung up and decided to go to the liquor store and come back to Big Lou's to give him more time. When I got outside, Crita was walking up to the car, looking back over her shoulder at Bones.

"Why you followin' me, man? You don't have noplace else to be?"

"Aw, Crita. Who you think followin' your flat behind?"

Crita stopped in front of the car. "Boy, I bet if I turn around, there ain't nobody there but you."

I didn't have to hide today. I stood right in front of the three of them and I was invisible. Crita reached for Babyback's beer and he let go of it without saying anything, as if it belonged to her. Bones asked, "You got a beer for me, Babyback?"

"What do I look like? Why I'm gonna be buying *you* beer?"

"Well, you could shove your damn beer up your ass, Babyback." Bones jabbed at the air. "I'll buy my own." He punched the air again. "And don't neither one o' you ask me for none neither."

"Ray Anthony ain't here yet?" Crita asked Babyback in her firecracker voice.

"Naw, he ain't here. Where's Geraldine?" Babyback whined.

194

"Geraldine say she don't wanna ride by herself with you, Babyback. Ain't nothin' I can do about it. She say you *too much* man for her." Crita doubled over and spit a spray of Babyback's beer across the hood of his car, laughing, or at least performing a laugh. He tried to snatch the can away from her, but she pulled away so that more of it spilled.

"Then it ain't no deal. You said if I let you an' Ray Anthony take a ride in my car without me, you'd get Geraldine to go with me. Now I ain't got nobody to drive around for myself and you think I'm gonna keep my part? What kinda chump you think I am?"

Crita walked up to Babyback and held the beer up under his nose. "I can't make Geraldine do nothin' with you she don't wanna do, Babyback. If you don't wanna let me an' Ray Anthony ride in your old piece o' car without you, then don't. Just remember I'm the one got Geraldine to even look at you twice. If you act like you got some sense, I *might* could get somebody to look at your pin-head self again."

Babyback froze, frowning down at her like an illustration I remembered from fifth grade of Gulliver glaring down at the Lilliputians. Crita stared right back up at him, holding the paper bag with the can of beer in it right up to his nostrils. Her bangs were sticking straight up like an overgrown crew cut.

"What am I supposed to do while you and Ray Anthony go drivin' off somewhere, Crita? Stand out here on the street, in the cold?"

Crita snapped, "That's what you been doin', ain't it?"

Bones came out of Big Lou's, holding a six-pack out in front of him. Crita laughed, thumbing in his direction. "And when Ray Anthony and me get through riding around, you and Bones can drive somewhere together."

I wanted to run and cut Ray Anthony off before he got to them, to ask him if he knew what they had planned for him. Him and Crita in the car alone together. He couldn't have known that once he got there, he'd have to drive around alone with this beerspitting loudmouth. I squeezed the cigarettes in my jacket pocket before I remembered what they were. Damn. I'd only stolen a couple. If they were broken, I'd buy more with Mom's money. I backed away, staring at Crazy Crita. I'd buy a pack of cigarettes for Ray Anthony and me. I had to have something to give him.

I went to the liquor store first. I got back to Big Lou's only a couple of moments before he strutted up to the front of the store.

29

Maybe he was dressed special for New Year's Eve. Maybe he was just in a good mood. Turquoise pants. Not blue, not green, but turquoise. High-water turquoise pants. They were so short I could see he had on those socks called Thick 'n' Thins, the nylon ones that looked half like men's socks and half like women's stockings. The socks were gray, the exact shade as his shoes. The shoes were patent leather, of course. How many pairs of patent leather shoes did Ray Anthony own?

Ray Anthony in turquoise was a surprise, even more of a surprise than in his purple pants and maroon shoes. I wasn't sure whether I thought he looked really good, in a Ray Anthony way, or like this time he'd gone too far. Crita didn't have to think about it.

"Who you think you sposed to be, Harry Belafonte or somethin'?"

It showed how stupid she was. As much as I wasn't sure what I thought about Ray Anthony in turquoise high-waters, I knew Harry Belafonte wouldn't be caught dead in them.

"I didn't think you was comin', man. Geraldine ain't comin'," Babyback whined, shifting his weight from side to side. Bones snickered. "Heh, heh." He leaned against the side of the store with a beer in his hand and an empty can at his feet.

"Babyback is still gonna let you an' me ride around for

a while. Ain't you, Babyback?" Crita stopped staring at Ray Anthony long enough to give Babyback this look that said, don't think about what to answer. Just open your mouth and say yes.

But Babyback didn't say yes. He shifted from side to side again, his nose running, his lips trembling from the cold.

Ray Anthony hadn't seemed to notice me since he got to Big Lou's. Every time he looked across the hood of Babyback's car I was staring right back at him, but he didn't look like he really saw me standing there feet away from where they all were.

Bones came toward the car. His eyes were a deep pink like the lining of his lower lip against his dark skin.

"Yeah, man. Whatcha say you, Crita and me take us a ride around, Ray Anthony? I let you drive."

"What?! You gotta be outcha mind, Bones," Crita yelled across the car at him. "I told you before, I ain't goin' nowhere with you. What me and Ray Anthony want you in the car with us for?"

Bones licked his lips slowly and smiled, one of those smiles that isn't about anything being funny.

"Man, I thought Geraldine was comin'." Babyback looked around him as if he was lost. "I thought we was gonna take turns. You and Crita. Me and Geraldine."

"I'm tellin' you, Babyback, forget Geraldine. I'll get somebody to ride with you, later. Me an' Ray Anthony wanna go ridin' now. Huh, Ray Anthony?" Crita combed her bangs down with her fingers and took a sip of her beer. Her hair stood back up as soon she'd taken her hand away.

Ray Anthony looked across the hood of the car and seemed to see me for the first time. He nodded and smiled. The rest of them turned around to see who had his attention.

"Ray Anthony?" Crita glanced at me and right back to him. She wanted an answer.

"Don't make me no difference," Ray Anthony said in his gravelly Creighton Heights Projects voice. "It's your car, Babyback. You the one to say who be drivin' it." He was talking with his back turned to them, still facing me but looking down at the car.

"Go on," Babyback said. He was running out of air, shrinking. "You an' Crita go on." Reaching into his pocket, he pulled out a ring of keys and held them in Ray Anthony's direction. "Here."

Crita grabbed another beer from the package and ran around to the side of the car where I was standing a few feet away. Bones stepped forward and snatched the keys out of Babyback's hand.

"I'll drive, man."

"Boy, I'm tellin' you, if you go, you be in that car by yourself!" Crita stepped away from the car door she'd started to open.

Bones raised the keys into the air, then slammed them down onto the hood of the car.

"Whatchu doin', man?!" Babyback sounded like Bones had hit him with the keys instead of the car hood. Bones went back to the front of the store and kicked the brick wall. Then he growled at it and kicked it again.

Ray Anthony was watching the whole thing like a storm was swirling around him and here he was in the middle, not moving, not even swayed. He walked closer to the car and took the keys from the hood. He said to Babyback, "I'm tellin' you man, it don't make me no difference."

Babyback looked from him to Crita. As if he was read-

199

ing instructions he saw in her eyes, he told Ray Anthony
again, "Go on. You and Crita. Go on."

Crita started to climb into the car. Ray Anthony
opened the blue door on the driver's side and stopped,
looking over at me. "You want a ride home?"

Crita spun around toward me and back to Ray
Anthony again. I was too surprised to say anything, but I
did want to be in that car with him, going home or anywhere he wanted to drive.

"C'mon," he said. "Get in."

Crita sucked her teeth loudly. "Ray Anthony, whatchu
doin?! You *know* him?"

"Sure, I know him. I'm gonna give him a ride home."
Ray Anthony smiled at me and I smiled back. I slid into
the backseat, with the liquor store bag in my lap.

He rolled his window down and asked Babyback,
"Whatcha gonna do while we gone?"

"Just don't leave me out here all day, man."

Ray Anthony rolled the window back up and pulled
away from Big Lou's.

"I got you a beer. You want me to open it for you?"
Crita asked him.

"I don't want no beer."

"Well, it's here if you want it."

It amazed me how fast Crazy Crita could make herself
sound like somebody's wife going on a picnic to Wil-
lowood Park in the family car, considering what was
really going on. I stared out the window as if we were
passing through some fascinating unknown territory
while Crita turned around in the front seat and looked at
me the same way.

"How long you been knowin' him?" she asked Ray
Anthony as she watched me.

"For a while now." He was still using the thick, foggy voice. I wondered how long he could keep it up.

"Huh!" Crita snorted. Now it was me she wanted an answer from. "Whatchu got in the bag?"

I was hoping not to have to say anything to her. I knew I couldn't sound afraid, and I couldn't sound stupid enough to think I could be friends with her either.

"It's scotch. For my mother."

"Your mother drink scotch, huh?"

No, I wanted to tell her, she cleans the oven with it. "Yeah," I said instead and tried to imitate the voice Ray Anthony was using.

"His mother got him buying scotch for her," she reported back to Ray Anthony. She hadn't thought of any way to make trouble for me and she was running out of time. We were a block from the parking lot where he would let me off. Surprised at how well I was doing, I opened my legs a little to look more relaxed and called to the front, "Ray Anthony, you got a cigarette?"

He looked up at me suddenly, frowning into the rearview mirror.

"What?"

I asked him again, trying to sound as if I was used to asking him for cigarettes, like it only made sense that if I'd run out, I could get one from him.

"Yeah. I got a cigarette." I could see he was still frowning, but he reached inside his jacket pocket and took out a pack of Pall Malls. He handed them over his shoulder to me.

"Thanks." I took one and handed the pack back to him, our eyes meeting again in the mirror. He was looking at me like he didn't recognize me. He slowed down near the entrance to the parking lot.

"I guess I'll save it for later, since we're here already."

Crita laughed one of her loud hatchet laughs. "Sissy boy, you need to give that man his cigarette back. You know you don't smoke nobody's damn cigarettes."

To hell with her. I wasn't going to answer. I reached for the door handle, but Ray Anthony didn't stop like I expected. He sped up, away from the parking lot.

"Whatchu know?! Huh, Crita?! You don't know nothin'!" It was his own voice now, higher, sharper. "You need to keep your mouth shut sometime."

I sat back, wishing he had let me get out. I was embarrassed to still be there after what she'd called me in front of him, but I was too afraid of her to say anything for myself. I couldn't even face Ray Anthony in the rearview mirror. I stared at the back of Crita's thick neck and tried to get up enough courage to ask him to let me out or to jump out without asking at the next stoplight. The three of us rode in silence across town.

"You mad?"

It was her wifey voice again. Ray Anthony had turned onto a street that led to the thruway and I thought about Mom waiting for me to come back from Big Lou's. Crita inched over toward Ray Anthony.

"Lemme see if you mad." She reached across to his lap. I pictured her grimy hand on his beautiful, turquiose-covered thigh.

"You ain't mad." She laughed. "I knew you weren't mad."

Ray Anthony looked up at me in the rearview mirror. We were on the thruway in the lane that said "Fairview Cove." He was driving to the south side, to the beach. On the last day of December.

• • •

There were only two other cars on the parking ramp overlooking the water. One of them drove off a minute after we parked. Behind us was the Fairview Cove Drive-In screen. The cement poles with speakers on either side of us looked like an army of naked blue children with huge ears waiting for someone on the screen to tell them what to do. I'd been to the drive-in twice. The last time we'd gone to a Kirk Douglas movie I forgot the name of. Mom bribed Ben into driving us by promising to pay for everybody, including him. On the way, they argued about moving. Mom asked Ben why she never heard him talk about wanting to get his family out of the projects as badly as she did. When we got to the drive-in, Ben told Mom, "Put the speaker on your side. You're the one who hears what you want to hear. Maybe you should get one of these to go in your new house." Mom started banging the speaker on its stand. "You ruin everything, you know that? Even when I pay your way, you can't have a good time unless you ruin it for everyone else." When the people around us started to stare into our car, I hid under the blanket in the backseat. Mom and Ben shouted at each other about not being able to leave because we were in the middle of hundreds of other cars and couldn't get out.

Staring behind me at the drive-in screen, I tried to figure out why Ray Anthony had driven both me and Crita to Fairview Cove, like it made sense to him for the three of us to be there together. She leaned up over the backseat and smiled down at me.

"You can get out and smoke your cigarette now."

I thought, if I get out, she'll convince Ray Anthony to

drive away and leave me here. I looked up at the rearview mirror. He was looking out at the beach.

"Well? Get out. Ray Anthony, tell Sissy Boy to get out the car and wait."

"I ain't tellin' nobody nothin'," he snapped at her.

"I'm gonna take off all my clothes. You think I'm gonna take 'em off in front of him?"

Ray Anthony took a toothpick out of his jacket pocket and started to pick his teeth, but he still wasn't looking at her. "That's up to you."

"Well here I go, then." When she unzipped her jacket, I jumped out of the car.

After a few minutes, I stole a look back. It was like watching pieces of a jigsaw puzzle move up, then over, sinking out of sight again. His back, wider than I'd imagined. The outline of her hair, his fist hitting the horn. I heard her rusty blade laugh. Then suddenly he shouted something at her I couldn't understand. Or didn't want to, because it sounded as if he was calling both our names at the same time and I was on the outside, not in there with him to separate mine from hers. Whatever he shouted, the part that sounded like he was calling me shot down into the pit of my stomach, no, deeper, deeper, and stayed there, aching.

Later, I told myself I couldn't have seen anything. I'd been watching the blank white drive-in screen, trying to remember the name of the Kirk Douglas movie and how long it took us that night to get out of there.

"Hey. C'mon."

Ray Anthony'd rolled down the window and practically whispered to me. I got back in the car and closed my eyes. It smelled, not bad exactly, but a smell that was the two of them together and didn't include me. I opened my window until we got to the thruway. It felt like we were riding in a convertible with the top down in the middle of winter. Over her shoulder, Crita snapped, "Shut it," and I did.

I don't know if Ray Anthony looked at me at all on the drive back. I didn't watch the rearview mirror to find out. When we got to the north side, he drove toward Stratfield Projects.

"What the hell do you think you're doin'? You drive me back to Creighton first." Crita glared at Ray Anthony until it was clear he'd changed directions. It surprised me she wanted to get out before me. I thought she'd be glad to get rid of me. When we got to Creighton Avenue, she told Ray Anthony to stop. She opened the door and turned to him, leaning in close enough to kiss him good-bye.

"That mess you done back there at the drive-in? That wasn't nothin'." Ray Anthony didn't look at her. She moved closer, as though he was hard of hearing. "It wasn't shit."

He shifted his toothpick from one side to the other. Slowly, Crita stepped out and slammed the door so hard, the car shook. Just before Ray Anthony pulled away, she smiled at me in the backseat. It was the smile from the dream I'd had, the smile that said, "You're lucky I'm letting you get away."

"I gotta go back to Big Lou's," I told Ray Anthony. I thought I'd start with the shopping and figure out the rest, like what to tell Mom. Babyback was still there in front of the store when we drove up, shivering and blowing into his palms. When I jumped out of the car, he looked surprised to see I'd been in it all the time.

I'd almost forgotten Mom's scotch. When I turned around to get it, the empty bag was on the floor, but the bottle wasn't. I tried to slam Babyback's car door harder than Crita had and dared either one of them to say anything about it.

"Louis." I didn't remember Ray Anthony ever calling me by my name before, and now, the first time he did, I was too furious to answer.

"Take this." He was holding rolled-up money out the window. I went around to him and snatched it from between his fingers.

"It ain't my fault," he said. For the first time, I didn't care what he said.

I went to the back of Big Lou's to the pay booth and called Mom. It barely rang before she answered.

"Mom—" I started. Beginning a lie you don't know the end of is like diving. You just go to the end of the board and jump, because if you wait too long, you ruin any chance of it turning out good. "I'm at Big Lou's, Mom, but there's a really long line and I went to the liquor store once, but I have to go back again."

"You're at Big Lou's?"

"Yeah, Mom."

"Are you alright?"

"Yeah, I'm alright."

I was in the middle of the air with the water waiting under me when I heard her crying.

"God, Louis. I was so afraid. I thought you were . . . I thought you . . . went away."

I remembered how tight she'd hugged me when I got off the train from New York. I still didn't know what Grandaddy had told her or what she thought I'd told him. The point was, I didn't have to lie about where I'd been instead of shopping for our New Year's Eve together. She was relieved to know I'd be there with her and for the moment that was all she cared about. That much, I guessed, was good luck. Watching Babyback driving Ray Anthony away, I wondered what kind of luck it was that I felt him watching me through the window. When I looked at him, he nodded the same as he had before, but this time neither one of us smiled.

Mom and I never really talked about where I'd been. I volunteered that I'd met a classmate who wanted to know about Ben's funeral and how I'd stood there in the cold outside Big Lou's and reported all the details to him. I knew Mom didn't believe me, but it didn't matter. She opened the bottle of scotch as soon as I gave it to her and had a drink and a cigarette. She glanced at me a few times as if she was actually listening to me lying to her, but I could see that wherever she'd gone in her head for the hours I was with Ray Anthony and Crita had worn her out. Now that I was home again she could rest and if she was listening at all, it was probably to record the lie.

That night, for the first part of her New Year's Eve party, the three of us ate lamb chops and mashed potatoes in the living room on trays in our laps. We watched *The Great Ziegfeld*. Mom did her imitation of Luise Rainer's French accent sighing, "Oh, Flo!" while I mouthed it. Even though I knew I could do it better, I didn't dare compete with her.

After dessert, Lorelle fell asleep with her head in my lap. That was my excuse for not dancing with Mom when Guy Lombardo's New Year's Eve special came on. But Mom woke her up anyway, singing "Let old acquaintance be forgot" and crying when the New Year came in. I looked across the courtyard. There was a light up on the fifth floor in Ray Anthony's mother's living room.

"What are you looking at?" Mom asked. "Aren't you going to drink your champagne cocktail?" She held up the glass she'd chilled for me and filled with ginger ale and a capful of scotch.

"I'm looking at the New Year," I told her. "Happy New Year," I whispered, looking up at the window across the projects courtyard. "Happy New Year."

30

"Raay-Raay! Sweet, sweeet Sugar Raay! Come on down here, Ray Anthony sweetie!"

It was early, a few minutes after eight, but I was definitely awake. I heard her as loudly as if she was outside our door calling *my* name. I pulled on a sweater, pants and my shoes and ran downstairs. Mom was smoking a cigarette, watching out the window but standing over to the side so she couldn't be seen. She looked like she was trying to avoid getting shot.

There was Crita in front of 4B with Bones and a boy I didn't know. All of her hair was sticking straight up all around like porcupine quills. Otherwise, she looked almost the same as she had the day before, except her jacket was open so I could see her pink blouse hanging over her pants. She had on the same dirty sneakers with no socks and holes that made me cold just looking at them.

"Shuuugarrraaay!" she yelled again. She threw her head back and her arms stretched out and jerked around in the air. "Ain'tchu comin' out, Raaay Aanthooneee? I got some boys down here for you to play with!"

Part of me wanted to run back upstairs. I didn't want to be in the room, knowing my mother was observing every detail, but I had to stay. I had to be a witness to this, I had no choice.

"I *said* I brought you some *boys* to play with, Ray

Anthony Robinson! Cause you like *boys* so much, you punk faggot!"

Bones shoved his friend and they both stumbled around in the snow, howling. Crita put her hands on her hips and repeated slowly, "You punk faggot!"

"Geez!" Mom whispered like she was watching a car accident. Her lips curled in disgust, she stuck her cigarette between them and took a deep, long drag. I wanted to tell her to go away, I'd report everything that happened, but I couldn't say anything. That morning, Mom was probably the only woman in the projects who worried about being seen snooping. As Crita continued to yell up to the fifth floor, I could see people on all the other floors looking down to the courtyard from their windows. Where was Ray Anthony? His mother's shade was down. Was he up there standing behind it? Were they both there?

"Come out here, punk! Whatchu doin' up there?"

Crita was punishing him. I remembered her smile when she got out of the car. I hadn't been wrong.

Bones reached down and gathered some snow. I closed my eyes. Please, God. Don't let them be that stupid. But he and his friend started hurling snowballs at the window while Crita continued to shout. From the time I'd first heard her to the second the 4B door flew open seemed like hours, but the moment I saw Ray Anthony, time suddenly sped up and I could barely keep track of what was happening.

"Get the hell away from here, y'all! Get the hell away!"

His voice was high, torn sounding, like a choked trumpet. He was wearing an undershirt, sleeveless, and his purple pants, patent leather shoes.

Crita ran to him. "You want a boy, faggot?! I brought you a damn boy!" She swung at Ray Anthony's head, but he stepped out of her way. "Get him, Bones!" she snarled. "Get him!"

Bones threw up his fists and danced toward Ray Anthony, grinning. "Heh, heh. Come on, punk. I always knew you wasn't nothin' but a punk. Come on."

Ray Anthony's arm shot out into Bones's face so suddenly, both Mom and I jumped like it was us who'd been punched. From then on, he hit him without stopping. He hit him until Bones started to sink. The whole time, Crita hollered, "Get him, Bones!" as if she was blindfolded and couldn't see what was really happening a foot in front of her.

By now, people had come out of their apartments and crowded in a circle around the three of them so it was harder for me to see what was going on. Mom and I were at opposite sides of the window, dodging from side to side, trying to follow the movement of the bodies. I didn't see Crita get behind Ray Anthony, but suddenly, she was on his back with her legs circling his waist, her arm around his neck like a hangman's noose. Bones got up. He was too weak to hit Ray Anthony very hard, but now his friend jumped in and the two of them beat him at the same time.

Ray Anthony went down backwards and Crita tumbled to his side. Bones's friend pushed him onto Ray Anthony. Bones sat on Ray Anthony's chest, hammering into his face.

I don't remember running out of the apartment and across the courtyard. Or pushing through the circle of people watching Bones carve into Ray Anthony's eyes and mouth with his fists. Afterwards, Miss Odessa told Mom it looked like I had the strength of a grown man twice my size when I threw myself against Bones and knocked him over.

Ray Anthony staggered to his feet again, his eye bloody and sagging. Bones rolled over to try to get up too, but Ray Anthony was too fast for him. He pulled Bones's head from the ground with both hands. Then he began to pound it against the concrete step outside 4B.

Ray Anthony's mouth twisted into a thick line of rope from ear to ear. But what I first thought was anger in his eyes, I suddenly recognized as something different. Something I'd seen in my mother's eyes, and my own. But I'd never seen it in Ray Anthony's before. I'd never seen fear in his eyes.

Maybe it had nothing to do with Bones. Maybe he was afraid because of what Crita had yelled, afraid someone might believe her. Maybe he was afraid for himself, afraid he really would rather be in a car with me than her. Had he called her name in the car, or mine? What I knew for certain was that Ray Anthony would beat Bones until he didn't feel afraid anymore, no matter how long it took or how much of Bones's skull he had to split open.

I jumped onto Ray Anthony like he was a speeding car, punching him with a strength I'd never felt before. But he didn't seem to know I was there at all. When he wouldn't let go of Bones, I bit into his shoulder. Hard. "Don't. You're going to kill him. Don't kill him, Ray Anthony. Don't."

I held on to him until he blurred in front of me. I don't remember letting go.

When the cops called the ambulance, they had to make the crowd stand back so they could get the stretcher through, the same as they had not two weeks before with Ben. It was a longer walk for them this time, from the parking lot to the courtyard and back. When they carried Bones away, half the projects followed as if what happened to him really mattered to them. The other half lagged behind, choosing to follow Ray Anthony and Crita to the police car instead.

Mom was making sure the cops didn't take me. Shoving her way through the crowd, she pulled me away from Ray Anthony and tried to block me from them. Ray Anthony stared at me like I was some stranger who'd run up to him out of nowhere, jumped him and bitten into his shoulder.

"Keep your white hands off me," Crita spat at the cop who tried to pull her along by her jacket collar. When he took her arm instead, she paraded to the police car, enjoying herself. Bones's friend claimed he'd only tried to break up the fight, but the crowd pushed him away from them toward the cops yelling, "Liar! Liar! Take him, too! Take him!"

Where was Ray Anthony's mother? When they handcuffed him, the shades on the fifth floor were still down. If she hadn't come by the time they drove him away, who would even know where they were taking him?

Watching for his mother is what kept me from running along beside him like everyone else was as they were taking him away. It's how I saw the silver key chain with the red rabbit's foot and the nail clippers on it. It must've fallen out of his pocket during the fight. I grabbed it out of the snow and ran toward the parking lot. Mom called to me not to go, but it sounded as if she was a thousand miles away.

The ambulance had just pulled off wailing and Crita and Bones's friend were already in the back of one of the police cars. Crita was smirking through the window. The two cops were about to shove Ray Anthony into a second car.

"Ray Anthony!"

I ran, holding the red rabbit's foot out to him. "I found it! It fell out of your pocket!"

Everyone was watching. The cops, the people from the projects. Watching and listening, as if I'd found important evidence and everyone was waiting to see what it would mean.

Ray Anthony's eye was bleeding badly. His shoulder, where I'd bitten him, looked like he'd been stabbed. My legs trembled. I didn't feel like the person who'd hurt him only minutes before.

"Here."

They'd cuffed his hands, so I tried to put his rabbit's foot in his pocket.

"Uh-huh. You. You keep it. See does it bring ya any luck."

I wanted to get him his leather jacket so he'd be warm, to ask the cops where they were taking him so he couldn't just disappear. I wanted to go with him. I could make things different because I knew the truth and could explain it.

But all I did was watch like everyone else when they pushed Ray Anthony down into the backseat with his hands locked behind him. They folded him up like cardboard. A big brown cardboard cutout of a man with a thick cloud of nappy hair the color of brick, wearing patent leather shoes. They folded him up into the back of their car. Then they drove him away from me.

31

I stayed in my room, avoiding Mom's questions and trying to figure out what the police could charge Ray Anthony with. Twice, Miss Odessa came to the apartment trying to sniff out a story she could take with her from door to door. A few minutes before noon, Mom called me from downstairs. I grabbed *Ivanhoe* and took it with me to give the impression it was important for me to get back to it as soon as possible. Mom was in the kitchen, sitting at the table.

"I was reading," I announced to her.

"You can go back to it. I just wanted to tell you"—she stopped and pushed an envelope on the table toward me—"*this* came for you yesterday."

I didn't recognize the handwriting, but it had more stamps on the envelope than on any letter I'd ever been sent. The postage mark said, "Jamaica, West Indies." I knew immediately who it was from.

"Yesterday?"

Why had Mom waited? I turned the envelope over. Had she read it already? Had she thought about not giving it to me at all?

"I meant to give it to you. I forgot. I was upset yesterday. Remember?"

I tried to grab my letter from the table as casually as I could and keep myself from running for the stairs. I got halfway up when she stopped me.

215

"Louis, who do you know in Jamaica?"

I started to answer without turning around at all, but I thought better of it.

"I think it's probably from Dr. Davis. She's a therapist at Burgess."

I wanted to say "*my* therapist," that's what came to me, but I knew what I'd said was safer.

"Why the hell is she writing you letters?"

"I don't know why she wrote me. I'll have to read it to find out."

It was the kind of answer I could have been knocked down for. Instead she said, "Just remember whose house you live in. She's writing letters to the house where *I* pay rent. I don't have to receive any mail I don't want to receive."

With that, she turned and walked back into the kitchen. I jumped the rest of the stairs two at a time, ran into my room and locked the door behind me as quietly as possible.

It wasn't a letter. It was a postcard inside an envelope. I was sure Dr. Davis had mailed it that way so I'd feel like I had some privacy. The front of it was sliced down the middle on an angle by a green line and on either side of the line was a different photograph. One photograph was of two dark brown women wearing bright blue dresses, with white smiles and their arms around each other dancing in the street at night. On the other side was a picture of sand almost as white as the women's smiles and beyond it, water that matched their dresses. The sand reminded me of being at the beach with Ray Anthony and Crita. The card said, "Happy Holidays. I'll see you soon. Dr. Davis."

It was all printed out in neat, black, block letters. Neat. That was the word. I'd been trying to figure out what happened when I talked to her that made me feel different when I came out of her office. That was it. Everything felt neater. It was all still there inside of me, all the things I'd told her and all the things I hadn't. But it felt like I'd sorted them out and put things in different piles. She was good at that. Her postcard made me think she must be good at it for herself, too.

I looked at the space above her name where she could have written "Love." I guess if she had, it would have seemed unprofessional, especially if somebody else had seen it. But I knew that's what she meant. I was sure of it. She meant "Love."

I got the book she'd given me and opened to where Ray Anthony had written his number. I knew the number, I'd just never connected him and Dr. Davis in any way before. It was okay that he'd written in the book she'd given me. She would have thought so too.

I wanted to call Ray Anthony's mother and ask her if she knew if he was in jail and did she have a lawyer? When they'd carried Bones away, he was unconscious, but that wasn't dead. They couldn't keep Ray Anthony if Bones wasn't dead, could they? How could they keep him in jail for fighting him? People fought each other all the time in the projects, but nobody got arrested for it unless they killed somebody. Were the cops so sure Bones was going to die?

It was the phone that woke me. I'd been going over the details of the fight in my head and I must've fallen asleep. I could hear Mom on the phone. A few minutes later, she called me. I jumped up and went out to the head of the stairs. Maybe I'd jumped up too quickly. The bottom of the stairs seemed to be moving. Rippling, black linoleum waves. I couldn't catch my breath.

"Yes, ma'am?"

"Odessa called." Mom waited until she'd turned on the hall light to finish, to make sure she could see me before she continued.

"Somebody saw the Robinson boy coming down Hicks Street. Police must've let him go. He must not've killed that other hoodlum like he was trying to."

I ran downstairs and past her, outside.

"Don't go back out there!" she shouted. "You want him to knock *your* head against some concrete?!"

When I got to the parking lot, I thought he must still be on Hicks Street, because I couldn't see him yet. Miss Odessa wasn't the only one who knew he was coming. There were already other kids standing at the edge of the lot looking up Hicks, yelling, "Here he comes! Here he comes!"

I stopped as though a wall suddenly dropped in front of me. I looked back toward the apartment where I knew my mother was still standing in the doorway. She wouldn't go inside and pull down the shade, no matter what happened now. She was waiting like everybody else was and she'd want to see what my part would be this time.

When I turned toward Hicks Street again, he was there in the parking lot. In his undershirt, bare arms hanging, fists at his side still stained with blood. He wasn't strutting this time. He was cold, for one. He had to be cold. His whole body looked as hard as his fists. No roundness. Just lines and angles. He walked as though he'd been gone for more than hours, more than days maybe. It was as if he'd come back after months of walking in the wind without a shirt or jacket and socks. Even his red hair seemed darker, muddied.

"Hey, Ray Anthony!" one of the younger boys called out. "They put you in jail?"

Ray Anthony looked up like he hadn't noticed anybody was in the parking lot but him. He didn't answer. But by this time, there were already more kids, keeping their distance like he was a dog they knew might attack without warning.

"You kill that boy?" one of them called to him.

Ray Anthony shook his head slowly from side to side. "Naw, I ain't killed nobody."

I pictured my mother again, still on the stoop outside our apartment.

I walked up close to Ray Anthony.

"Hi," I said, softer than I wanted to. Neither one of us stopped moving.

"How you doin'?" he asked me in a voice that was almost as soft as my own, only lower and I thought, he's afraid, he's still afraid.

But as he spoke to me, his walk began to change. It was slower, easier. It was almost the walk my mother had seen from our living room window, the one I liked to watch before he knew I was watching.

There were more kids once we got into the projects. Quickly, I glanced out of the corner of my eye across the courtyard. Bubba Graves was there. And Rat. All of them, there to witness. In front of our apartment standing next to Miss Odessa, Mom was waiting. I clamped my teeth together. Ray Anthony reached into his back pocket, pulled out a chewed-up toothpick and slid it between his lips. Reaching into my own pocket, I felt his rabbit's foot. I held it between my fingers, against my thigh, before I had to give it back.

I must have had my eyes closed, because I didn't see what happened next. I felt it. I was thinking how when we got to 4B, Ray Anthony would go in alone. I'd run across the courtyard, past Bubba and Rat, past my mother and that imbecile Miss Odessa and back inside. My mother could do whatever she wanted, once I was home.

But it was when I was pulling the rabbit's foot out of my pocket that I felt Ray Anthony's hand on my shoulder. Not around it, but on it, as if he was using it to help him walk. Except he wasn't. I could tell by the way it felt. It was only there for a second, but when he took it away there was no mistaking it had been there.

I looked up at him and he smiled. I could see just the edge of his chipped tooth and the cleft in his chin widen a little.

"You embarrass' to be walkin' with me?"

"No. No," I said as quickly as I could. "Are you?"

"Hell no," he told me, almost singing it, rolling the toothpick to the other side with his tongue. "Whatchu think?"

And I didn't know what I thought, because for once I didn't want to think at all. So I did what I'd wanted to do for a long time. I just walked. I walked across the Stratfield Projects courtyard with Ray Anthony Robinson in his purple pants and his patent leather shoes. And I remembered and knew. Remembered his hand on my shoulder. And knew it would be there again.

Can you feel the floor, Louis? Can you feel the floor?
  Yes. I can feel the floor.
  Of course, I can feel the floor. . . . Whatchu think?

How sweet, how sweet to save and be saved.

SUNDAY YOU LEARN HOW TO BOX

DISCUSSION QUESTIONS

1. When Louis first sees Jackie Wilson singing on television, he is taken by the passionate words and music about love and danger (page 47). What is the relationship between love and danger in Louis's life? What does he risk by loving his mother? Ben? Ray Anthony?

2. For most children, learning to ride a bike is an initiation rite, taking them from childhood to adolescence. If this is so, what is the significance of Ben allowing the other boys to take turns riding Louis's bike before he learns how to ride it himself?

3. After a fight between Louis and Ben, Louis's mother says to him, "Don't ruin what I'm trying to do" (page 74). What is she trying to do? How does her marriage to Ben figure into her goals? What does she expect from him? From Louis?

4. What is Jeanette's vision of a family? What is family supposed to achieve in her view? How does her past contribute to her view? Do you believe she attains her goal? If not, what do you think prevents her from achieving her ideal?

5. Why does Louis deliberately engage the photographer from the *Stratfield Journal*? Does he really hope to reach other kids who may be crazy? Or does he want to embarrass his mother and Dr. Shapiro? Does he just need attention (page 122)?

6. There is considerable pressure on Louis to "act like a man." What does that mean in his neighborhood and family?

7. Louis is fearful of the boys in the neighborhood, yet finds the courage to speak to Ray Anthony. What gives him this courage? Why does he feel drawn to Ray Anthony?

8. Why do you think Jeanette decides to send Louis on the train to visit with his grandfather in New York City? What is it about their personalities that keeps the two men from communicating? Does their relationship with each other develop over the weeks?

9. Why does Louis seek out Ed McMillan after the initial encounter on the train? Do you think he is drawn to Ed as father figure? A lover? A friend? Is he drawn to the danger?

10. How does Louis's relationship with Dr. Davis differ from the one he had with Dr. Shapiro? Do you think he feels more comfortable confiding in her? If so, what inspires this confidence?

11. Does your view of Jeanette change after she pierces Louis with a cooking fork? Is Jeanette now more of an enemy to Louis than Ben?

12. Can we accurately judge Jeanette's love for Louis by her actions toward him?

13. If you could change one thing about Louis that would make his life substantially easier, what would it be?

14. Based on what you know about Louis as a fourteen-year-old, what might the adult Louis Bowman be like?

15. Louis never really learns to box, but he does strike out, both figuratively and literally. What are some examples of his forays into adulthood? How does he reach a sense of self in an environment that tries to quash it? What does he really want from life?

ABOUT THE AUTHOR

Bil Wright was born in the Bronx, New York. He is a graduate of New York University (Tisch School of the Arts, Acting Major) and earned his M.F.A. in playwriting at Brooklyn College. While in graduate school, Bil worked at The Door, an internationally known walk-in center for adolescent youth. He taught English at New York's Housing Works, a service organization for men and women with H.I.V. Upon graduation from New York University, he became one of the directors of a special performing arts program at the Martin Luther King Center for Social Change. He has taught English Composition E.S.L. and literature at Brooklyn College and Long Island University, and has taught acting at Marymount Manhattan College.

His plays have been produced at Yale University, Orchestra Hall in Detroit, Dixon Place, Nuyorican Café, and the Samuel Becket Theater in New York. His plays were published in the anthology *Tough Acts to Follow.* Another one of his plays, "Them There Eyes," received a reading as part of the Playwrights Horizons BLACK INK Playwrights Series and was later produced at HERE.

His fiction has been published in many anthologies, including *Men on Men* 3 and *Shade.* His poetry is anthologized in *The Road Before Us,* edited by Assotto Saint, *The Name of Love,* and *Jugular Defenses,* as well as the literary journals *The James White Review* and *Art and Understanding.*

Sunday You Learn How to Box is his first novel.

I have spent a good portion of my professional life either teaching or working in environments that were ostensibly structured to nurture the intellectual and social lives of people outside what society calls its "mainstream." The concept of a mainstream in America is provocative, considering how many groups of people fall outside of it. This makes for a very narrow mainstream with a good many Americans, because of race, economics, sexual orientation, or physical or emotional disadvantages existing presumably on either shore.

As a teacher of students struggling to increase their reading skills and adults living with HIV and AIDS, my students often comment on the dearth of characters they could relate to.

"Professor Wright, you never see us in these books. It's somebody's version of what they think we are, but most of the time, it's not really us."

I can't say that I wrote the book specifically for this group, but I definitely wrote it knowing that there are Louises in the world who might have found "the ring" of their environment a little easier had they seen themselves in print and understood that there were other kids in comparable situations struggling to get through. I hope readers will be able to identify with Louis and Jeanette, whom I feel very close to, because their relationship, in its own way, is very classic and yet their personalities and individual histories give them specificity.